MISSION AMERICA

MISSION AMERICA

Published in 2015 by YouCaxton Publications
www.youcaxton.co.uk
ISBN 9781909644885

Cover Artwork by Matt Coburn

MISSION
AMERICA

Michaela Burco

MISSION AMERICA

This story is based on the tribes of the Santee River (South Carolina) in 1526; and the Spanish explorers, who had a foothold on the Caribbean island of Hispaniola (Dominica). The chronicles of Peter Martyr, written at the time, give the Spanish names, but the First Peoples left no written record.

PROLOGUE

AXA

He trapped her in the black, filthy bowels of the ship. The thumping pulse in her ears blocked out the screeching timbers twisted by the sea. Each grunt brought him closer and he grabbed her, but she snatched his knife, cut his throat, and gorged on his blood until she made her escape. When she hit the water she did not look back, and marooned on the beach, only survival mattered.

Axa locked the memories away, but they could burst out of the vault at any time. Hunger and fever had ended, but the stench and wailing of the other captives came in terrible dreams. Were they being taken to the Underworld? Deep inside the nightmare, someone released her chains. In despair, she killed a sailor who attacked her, and they threw her overboard in a damaged sail. Had demons plunged her into hell and spewed her out?

With her first steps on dry land, she prayed this torture would not scar her for life, and that one day she would free the other captives.

* * *

Weeks later, Axa lay hidden in the forest, with the blanket of darkness giving way to daylight. Downwind, at the edge of a strange settlement, the low sun lifted a veil of mist to reveal the morning rituals of the local villagers. The hostess looked important - perhaps a queen - with three spirals painted on her smock, just like the cuts on Axa's forehead. Her breathing slowed, but she gripped the sailor's knife tightly in her hand. Why did his dagger have the same three-spiral symbol? Awful memories slapped her in the face and a red curtain fell over her eyes.

3

In the nitty-gritty of the ship, her attacker jumped in front of her. She fought for her life, but it ended quickly when her training took over... a knee to his groin... and an elbow-strike that broke his nose and knocked him out. Her other hand twisted the knife from his weakened grasp, before she pulled his beard and slashed under his chin. He barely groaned, and she gulped the spurting blood that slowed to a trickle as he slipped away.

Wincing in pain, she bit her lip breaking the skin. The grinning demons of her nightmares turned away, and she blanked out their carping voices for now.

Focus on the villagers. At last, people living a normal life... hope for the first time since her escape. The hostess in the clearing sipped animal blood from a cup, but not to keep her alive. The odour punched through the smell of flowers and livestock, while the sounds of birds and beetles smothered Axa's breathing and swept away her troubled thoughts. A group of children surrounded this queen, waiting on words and signs that were strange but still made sense.

"Settle down children," she ordered. "I will be with you in a moment, but first I must salute Father Sun."

The children relaxed in front of her.

"Our Father, give us our daily bread," they said together, also mixing their voices with signs. Several, no more than toddlers themselves, carried babies on their backs wrapped in sheets.

"Great sun and earth, give us your blessing every day," the queen chanted.

She drew symbols on the ground with a prayer stick and lifted painted sheets. Her leather dress, woven scarf, wicker belt, and jewellery all oozed craftsmanship. Even the children's clothes were clean and beautifully made.

Axa scratched at her clothes, hastily made from tough hide and stitched with sinew to protect her from thorns and bites. Living off the land had soon restored her health and wits. She had made a bow and quiver full of arrows using the sailor's knife, and a wooden weapon with three stabbing points in case of attack from predators.

Her lips pressed into a smirk - like a child again with no make-up, no duties, and playing endless hide-and-seek. She had cut her hair as short as possible, which used to be a sign of revolt when she ran away as a youngster, wild and free.

Free? Like the freedom to drift in that damaged sail. Barely floating in the green soup of the delta where the sailors had thrown her overboard. Freedom from chains, but only a fold in the canvas allowed her to breathe with her nostrils just out of the silty water. Who knew what flesh-ripping creatures patrolled that murky swamp looking for an easy meal, or waited in the mud at the shoreline to ambush their prey?

Snorting the nightmares away, she blinked hard to picture her captors on the ship, because the red skin of this new queen mimicked the sunburn of the sailors. In Axa's Ashanti tribe, her aunts told stories of these seafaring men.

"Little Princess, for centuries the Spanish came in their square-sailed ships, and they swapped flint for our hardwood and tin for our gold. Arabs from the east, who used three-pointed sails, also offered trade not war - at least in the beginning."

Nearby, she saw some men from the new village.

They had high cheeks and square jaws like the Arabs, but otherwise they were different, and taller than the Spanish. Ashanti legends never featured a place and a people like this.

A laugh welled up inside her as the queenly ritual became a fight.

"Children, children, take your turn," the queen shouted, but the orderly queue turned into a rabble.

"Mama, thank you for our daily bread." The youngsters smothered her in cuddles and grabbed the loaves next to her.

She could belong here. The first time she had felt this way since her capture, but what should she do? What did all these signs mean... signs of trade and signs of danger - like the weapons they carried? These people of the forest wore elaborate feathers and decorated clothes, with symbols that spoke to each other. Scouts called through the trees, while drums and songs carried messages between settlements. When they met on the trails, they greeted each other with gestures and touches.

Careful... they all had bows and arrows. Without warning, they fired these at birds and animals, and even hanging fruit. Were they showing off, or practicing for a fight? Should she follow her heart and make contact, or follow her head and slip away?

Curse fate, she had been an Ashanti princess with her life ahead of her. How had her jungle paradise turned into a place of shame, with chains on her hands and feet, and a sack over her head? Only her ears witnessed that part of her torment, as the clanking of the ship smothered the awful sound of captives being forced aboard. What curse brought her to that rat-infested bottom-deck, with fifty other victims and not a chink of light?

Axa's feelings swung from vine to vine - lifting, stalling and plunging again - but staying within her like a witch's brew. Then, with godly timing, the queen interrupted.

"Now children, there is Mother Earth to bless, as well as the ancestors."

The children duly settled again in front of her, calmed by the bread in their mouths and hands.

The queen chanted quietly, resting her hands on the spirals on her smock. Could this mystery woman share the power of the Three Spirals that linked the Clan Mothers of the whole world for all time? Axa normally trusted that symbol completely, but she could not be sure that it had the same meaning in this unknown place.

Not far away, on a trail into the settlement, two men crossed paths. Different tribal feathers and jewellery suggested they were from different clans. Leaning forwards, they touched foreheads, laughed, and embraced. Sailors shook hands to show they weren't going for their swords... was touching foreheads a similar ritual if the weapon was the bow and arrow?

Axa desperately wanted to trust this new people and not fear them, but what of her terrible time with the sailors? Her nightmares waited just inside her eyelids, so she could barely blink. She had to keep watching this woman, these children, and this settlement until she was sure they were more like her.

CADIZ

Rats shunned the courtroom in Santo Domingo, but infested the cells below where Marco had been in custody. After the slave girl escaped, his flotilla had returned to the island of Dominica - foothold of the Spanish empire in the New World. Shaking in the dock and facing the death sentence, he noted the charges - stealing the captain's knife, murdering a sailor, and losing a slave. The prosecutor had made a convincing case, but Marco defended himself with his last energies.

"My Lord, the murdered sailor stole the knife - from the Captain's quarters. The slave girl killed him, and she escaped by her own wits."

How had it come to this? With a hollow stomach and parched mouth, his hands quivered as he held the rail and his dwindling thighs twitched. What had happened to his mother's favourite son... spoiled with love on their farm in Castile.

The judge interrupted proceedings. "Give him a seat and some water."

Marco wobbled as an usher brought him a stool and a mug of dirty liquid. Grimacing from sitting on his bony haunches, he closed his eyes tight hoping it would all go away. He plucked at his filthy cotton shirt and pantaloons, and rolled his feet in his dry, cracked boots. Scratching his beard, he found matted fur spreading across his face. His greasy hair itched with nits, and licking his teeth, he tasted plaque.

Only the elderly judge, Governor Juan Toledo, stood between Marco and the gallows. He carefully stroked his silver beard, groomed by servants but lost in folds of skin, and he studied the feeble young man in the dock.

Another scapegoat for another failed voyage to the north, he thought to himself. Twenty-odd years ago, this defendant's father had discovered a land to the north of Cuba. Toledo sighed deeply. How long would it take to replicate the success of Cortes in New Spain, or at least find a seaway to the west?

A foghorn in the nearby harbour brought his attention back to the courtroom, but his many years in the colonies had left him weary. His fine robes couldn't conceal his worn-out soul as he summed up the case.

"The knife was stolen from the captain's quarters, the sailor's throat was cut from ear to ear, and compensation is due to the shipping company for the loss of the slave." He raised his voice at the word 'compensation', before returning to a sombre tone. "A death sentence would be appropriate for each of these, never mind all of them."

A few shards of light pointed accusingly at Marco, who sucked his cheeks and looked at the passers-by who had come in to see a man condemned to death.

His eyes flitted to the symbols of authority all around him, and noted how, in the pantomime of the court, each actor knew their part. Above all, a fresco of Lord God adorned the ceiling. Below the image of God, King Carlos - the Holy Roman Emperor - stared out from his painting in its gilded frame on the wall. Below the painting of King Carlos sat Governor Toledo, the judge, on his raised platform. Below him the lawyers, ushers, and escorts shuffled about. By piling their disdain upon him, one upon the other, all the symbols made Marco almost want to die.

"Only you as boson," Toledo said to Marco, "had keys to the captain's quarters and keys to the chains of the slaves."

Marco's sighs stirred the dusty air, mimicking the painted clouds around the Lord God himself. Even the squawking seagulls fell silent, and only the clanking of the rigging from the ships blew in through the windows.

Governor Toledo shuffled in his seat. This defendant was different. There were rumours he was an adventurer hoping to find gold in the new lands to the north. Certainly, he wasn't the usual uncouth boson with responsibility for disciplining some of the most unruly men on the sea. By his name and reputation, Marco de Serena was clearly higher-born, from a well-known family.

Marco turned his head and saw the leader of the expedition in question, Captain Cadiz, sitting in the gallery. Cadiz arrogantly sported the face hair of a conquistador, and his ginger-streaked beard gave him the appearance of a tiger. His blue and white striped shirt and his metal breastplate shone in the dingy courtroom.

Next to him on the rough-hewn benches sat an American Indian man, fiddling with a piece of paper. His immaculate skin stretched tight over a stony face and he wore his Spanish clothes awkwardly. A crucifix hung around his neck and he had removed his tribal ear studs.

"Luca... the letter," said Cadiz. The daydreaming Indian didn't reply. "Luca!" the captain grunted.

The Indian immediately sat upright.

Was Marco's freedom in the hands of this native? Praying hard, he stared at the note in the native's hand as if he could somehow change its contents. Could this letter be for the judge, perhaps providing an alibi? With the captain's rank, he could have the note slipped to the usher, who would take it to Toledo. Perhaps Cadiz wanted to claim a stake in any gold that Marco discovered. In the custom of the Spanish tribe, a favour was a debt of honour for life.

Cadiz coughed, Luca passed the letter, and after glimpsing at it, the judge continued.

"Despite all the evidence, on the counts of theft and murder I find you not guilty."

Marco collapsed in the dock and Toledo didn't give him time to find his feet.

"On the count of losing the slave, I find you guilty. You will be banished until you can compensate Captain Cadiz."

Marco looked into the gallery, but Cadiz and the Indian had already left. Holding back a wry smile, he asked to speak, and found the strength to perform the crucifix on his forehead and chest.

"My Lord, before God, I thank you for your mercy. I accept my debt to Captain Cadiz with gratitude."

He bowed low as the judge left the room, and his mind ran over his narrow escape from the death sentence.

It was a stitch-up, but Marco had given fate the slip. The sailor had stolen the knife, while Marco had been conspiring with the captive girl in a plan to find gold. He would need a guide to the wilderness and she would be trained in survival and sign language. Speaking enough Ashanti to explain his plans to her, he released her and smuggled her below.

The Celtic sailor had later found her and she killed him. Keeping the secret until they came to the anchorage, Marco had pretended to discover the body on his rounds. Before raising the alarm, he showed the girl how to conceal herself and be thrown into the water with the rubbish.

"I must return the knife," he had said, just before she had jumped ship. "It has great symbolic value to the captain."

Then her flaming eyes and skill with a blade had made him change his mind, but he hoped to find her somewhere in the wilderness.

PART ONE

CONTACT

ONA

Ona, the queen of the Santee People, drinks the blood in her goblet and she toasts the children sitting around her. They have been chattering eagerly about rumours of the black woman, though nobody in the village will admit to seeing her. This news splutters from the lips of Inca, a mixed-race boy with red hair and blue eyes, who is a talisman of the young group. He cannot keep up with the young hunters, but makes brews from herbs and insects and is often found in fevered dreams or being sick.

"Inca, what have you heard?" Ona says, as she sits cross-legged and he rushes around her.

"Great Ona, I would never eavesdrop on the lodge. If I heard the wizards talk of a black woman in the forest, I wouldn't tell anybody."

She touches his cheek, pale and freckled. How lucky the Santee are to have this puny lad as her grandnephew. She smiles, remembering his Celtic father had come with the Spanish many seasons ago, leaving a Spanish helmet that had become a prized trophy - showing her tribe's contact with the wider world.

"The legends," Ona says, "sing of the Inuit people to the north, and the Taino to the south. Could the black woman be one of those?"

"I wouldn't spy on the wizards, or talk about them speaking of a woman like you." He points to the three spirals on her smock - his blue eyes bulging from their sockets.

She glances into the middle distance to catch her thoughts. Could it be that this new woman is also a queen? If so, where is her clan? Even a nomadic queen migrates with her people. What of her strange body-paint and the spirals of which Inca speaks? She meditates for a moment about this new power in the wind, but isn't worried - there have been no portents of bad luck.

Inca watches quietly as she puts her hands together in a prayer-like pose, stretching every joint above her hips and reaching for the sky. That's better... there's nothing to fear... her hands flop back onto her lap. Nevertheless, such strange rumours will need further study.

She smells the men on the breeze, as they return from an overnight hunt. It is spring now – a time for trapping and growing – but perhaps the stories of harsher winters are true. The ice-gods do seem to be pushing the big grass-eaters down into the surrounding foothills.

"Winter is over," she chants quietly...

"Thank the bison and elk we followed.

Bless their carcasses for food and clothing.

Praise their cooking fat and medicine."

She picks up the Spanish helmet.

"Now Inca, the men are back, and it's time to put things away."

Inca runs around picking up blankets until hidden among them. The hallowed helmet, the blood goblet and her tea-making things also need to go back to the queen's tepee.

The dew is burning off, and the humming of the rapids mixes with the voices of the hunters as they come nearer. Ona smells a carcass - so there is a kill - but the men are muted and even sombre in their talk.

Leaving Inca and the others, she places herself in the power-seat near to her tepee. The rumblings of unhappiness from the men continue for a few prickly moments, and then Chet comes over, shoulders hunched.

Ona settles in the seat, mimicking his posture. Something is wrong. Chet is her most keen and faithful brave, but several of the mature hunters do worry too much. The old wizards sometimes struggle to calm their fears. Rumours always abound about hunting-grounds changing and other clans having new weapons to kill animals, but Chet never seems to be afraid. "Leave it to the wizards," he would say, "they will do the queen's bidding."

Today though, he smells worried.

"What news of our black queen?" Ona says calmly.

"Spirit of the shadows. Forgive me Clan Mother, how do you know about her? You are truly a great witch. It is true, there are sightings of the black woman in these parts and she smells sweet like our women... but why do you say 'queen'? There's no word of any tribe with her."

Doesn't he know about the spirals? Chet is a fine athlete, but many of the inner-circles within the men's lodge operate without his knowledge.

She squeezes all the old air out of her body. If Chet doesn't know about the spirals, then how does Inca know? Perhaps Inca is a better spy than she thought. Either way, even he would never joke about a thing like that.

LEGENDS

Axa ignores the beetle high-stepping across her face. Watching a young man visit the queen, her eyes flicker towards his muscular frame before her focus returns to the ritual and tribal life in general. This is a new land with unusual details, but there is so much that is familiar.

They are hunters and farmers, but traders too. Their clothing, pottery, and tools are made from things that aren't from this valley, or these mountains. They haggle in domed huts, holding meetings that go on late into the night. Scattered around are groups of tepee in motherly clusters, just like Africa. All around there is music from harps and drums, and play-acting as well as squabbling.

Her mind wanders back to the Clan Mothers in Africa, sharing stories of prosperity - but one story had a warning message.

"Princess Axa, we have so much gold that it holds little value for us, yet it is highly-prized by visitors. They think it is magical and will do anything to get it."

There is no gold on view in this new land, but there is art and custom. These people of the forest haven't chosen this site for defence, and there is no fortress. There are no hordes of weapons, like those now kept in Africa in case of attack.

One surprising sight makes Axa's tongue stick to her palate, as she gulps in disgust. This queen sits next to a Spanish helmet, which seems to have some high status too, and the children give it a wide berth while attending to her ritual needs.

Axa rubs her sweaty thumbs against her fingers, but it just makes them worse. Power of love, here is a new people in a new land, but with the Three Spirals from the Dreamtime. Then there is a helmet from the sailor tribes, who are from some future time, or another world altogether. Can any good come of this assortment of spirits? She drops her guard and demons flood into her mind with omens of tyranny and hatred, laughing and spitting contempt. Her stomach turns in horror and she curses their trespass.

Go to hell. Go to hell. Quick – focus on the real world and block out the invaders.

These red-skinned people farm corn and freshwater mussels... the evil spirits stop cackling.

Look - hunting, gathering and fishing... the monsters turn around.

There are pumpkins, beans, and sunflowers... the invaders trudge away, muttering curses, but she must make sure they keep going.

Children gather walnuts, plums, and seeds.... she curses her survival diet and yearns for these luxuries. The evil spirits do leave her mind, but her appetite will have to wait. With a rumble in her stomach, Axa rolls onto her back and briefly tries to melt into the fallen leaves beneath her. She remembers the noise of the ships fading into the distance, and the sounds of the forest cleaning her mind.

Foreign drums and callings had guided her inland, while carved or painted stones led her to this place. The accents in the drums were different and the tongue in the signs was new, but the same Earth Mother surrounded her here. Now, she is reborn from the awful womb of that ship, and she prays she will never see the monstrous world of the sailor tribes again.

Rolling back onto her stomach, she thinks of moving closer? Her own scent has changed after contact with the sailor tribe. Most of them were Spanish or Portuguese, but some bragged of coming from other places if the pay was good. Like all the sailors from the far north, the one that she had killed stank of milk. Does she smell like that, after swallowing so much of his blood? She sniffs herself frantically for a few moments.

These new people smell like her own Ashanti scent, and the men are respectful to the women - unlike the sailors. She slowly pulls her legs up into a ball and drops her head into her hands. Her scalp tingles and she flexes her toes. Forcing a yawn to stretch the agony from her face, she hears her mother's encouragement... "Trust in yourself, we trust in you".

Is it time to trust?

These new people worship the Overworld, they are well fed and warm-hearted. Beautiful symbols adorn their clothes and tepee. They trade widely, and they aren't prepared for war. Perhaps this is her chance to repair her life... to scorn the hell of her captivity... and to find a loving family like the one she used to have.

Then again, she can see that something is making the men nervous. Could it be Axa herself? There's no gold on view... but there is a Spanish helmet. These people could be in a truce with that greedy tribe.

Either way, what about the other captives... her kin? Can she forget their hell?

BEAR

Ona goes back towards her tepee but she is in a spell. The legend of a saviour sent by the ancestors is preying on her wits. She takes a charred nugget of wood from a fire pit and doodles on her forehead. Round and round it goes, in three spirals. 'A newcomer will one day save the First People from ruin.' Why was this legend only coveted by the queens of each tribe, and never shared with the rest of the elders? How would she know which newcomer, or when, and what ruin? Either way, this is too much for Chet and the others. She wipes the charcoal off her face before they see it, but the fable still circles her mind... a newcomer will save them from an abyss, a newcomer will save them from an abyss.

They belong to far-off worlds, but Axa is close enough to feel this unknown woman's aura. She delves into Ashanti myths and prays that the spirits of reason will guide her thoughts, but careful ghosts speak first.

'Beware of contact with new peoples. Women ruled in peace until the sailors came on horseback and everything changed. Trade turned to war, and they replaced their queens with greedy, brutal kings. A dangerous new era blacked out the never-ending cycles of the Dreamtime.'

Axa fights the angels of fear. The Three Spirals cannot be mistaken. She and this new queen share high status, a sweet smell, and peaceful motherly customs. Their peoples have mastered skills and resources and they seem to share a sense of humanity.

Spirits, say what she is thinking, Axa prays in the undergrowth.

Spirits, say why she is here, Ona demands silently as

she puts the ritual objects into her tepee.

'I will leave her a sign,' Axa resolves, 'and try to meet with her face-to-face.'

'I will leave her a sign,' Ona decides, 'in the hope of bringing us together.'

Axa's thoughts briefly leave her body behind, and her troubled mind. With fingertips gently massaging the spirals on her temples, her spirit swallows up her worldly life completely, and muses with endless time and space. Out there, she feels a oneness with this queen, but then, curse fate, she also senses a danger.

In the world of touch, sound, and smell, a large and hungry meat-eater is stalking her from down the wind. How did she allow her guard to drop? The heady sight and sound of the other queen have allowed the giant predator to surprise her.

A split second later Ona sounds the alarm, with shrill yelps defying the grunts of the charging animal. In moments, the whole village are at the edge of their camp armed with bows and spears.

"Chet, you take the legs. I will take the eyes," Ona commands in a loud, unruffled voice.

"Yes my queen," Chet calmly raises his spear and flexes his shoulders. "Great Eagle, fly with me on this one," he adds quietly, as he strokes the feathers worn on his belt.

They all watch in amazement as the great bear looms at a gallop, faster than a deer. It charges straight at them, holding its head and eyes perfectly stable - set on their invisible target. Everybody raises weapons and their eyes focus, ready to unleash a volley of precisely aimed arrow and spear points.

The animal bolts sideways, first right then left, in an

ungainly double sidestep.

"What spirit is this?" Chet rocks back. "Is it the Morning Star?"

The rest of the village shares his bemusement, but his reference to the spirits is reassuring. With all eyes on the bear, no one has seen the wisp of movement as a dark figure springs from nowhere and vanishes into the trees.

The ghost is Axa. Her heart stops at the sight of this hairy beast, but a shimmy - this way and that - makes it change direction twice to chase her. She has a small head start. Her body burns with energy but she coldly pictures an escape route. Running freely through the chest-high grasses, she finds the low cliff that separates the village from the beaches of the great river nearby. Any hunting animal can run her down on the flat, but not down a slope! Just as the bear's spit flicks towards her thighs, she plunges down the cliff towards the river.

Springing off the clay, she gets the lead she needs to shimmy again, spin round, and strike. The beast side-steps and Axa leaps onto its shoulders, scooping the fur under its chin as it tries to bite her. With one arm round its neck, rousing the spirits of rage, she slices the animal's throat from ear to ear using the blade in her other hand.

She has sharpened the sailor's knife for many hours, so arteries spurt blood and veins spew gore over the bear's matted coat. Axa rolls off its giant shoulders, straight into a running stride down towards the shingle and the rapids. Without a backward glance, she plunges into the churning river that sweeps her invisibly from the scene.

IDOLATRY

"Have you NOTHING to show for this expedition? One ship sunk on the return voyage, with horses and slaves lost. The investors are very disappointed."

The accountant hunches over documents piled up on his desk. He and Captain Cadiz glow from the sunset over Santo Domingo harbour, pouring in through a small window.

Cadiz straightens. He's not used to criticism from pen pushers. He strums the cracked varnish of the desk and a fist of annoyance sits low in his gut. With a sneer of his moustache, he dismisses it. Everything is under control.

"Sir," Cadiz says, "The reconnaissance was successful, and the friar celebrated mass with the Indians who canoed to our vessel. Some were converted and will spread the word of God in the new lands."

The accountant looks at Cadiz over his spectacles. He knew the captain from many years earlier, when they worked together for Christopher Columbus.

Thirteen years ago, he and Cadiz had also worked under Captain De Leon, charting the Bahamas. They didn't find its gold, or its famous fountain of eternal youth, but steered north-west and landed in the east of Florida. He remembers Cadiz the navigator, declaring this an island, and now the damn fool was trying to sail round it.

An Indian enters the room after a brief struggle with the door handle. When the expedition led by Cadiz hadn't found a safe anchorage, the Indian had apparently come aboard and volunteered to be a translator. There were rumours he had travelled with a number of Spanish expeditions and been to Spain, where he was baptised as

'Luca de Chicora', after the name of his tribe.

"Luca, welcome." Cadiz offers his seat and flicks his sword round to his hip. Pacing back and forth, he booms out, "Tell him about six six six - the sign of the devil."

The last rays of the sun go out like a light.

Cadiz stops strutting and snorts loudly to confirm his menace. His big, black shape turns slowly towards Luca, and he continues in a solemn tone.

"You must bear witness to the evil in these Indians. Three sixes - the number of the beast – it was carved on that girl's scalp, and you said they will make her a queen."

A few hours later, Cadiz sees Luca wandering the downtown area of the port and invites him into a bar off a side street. He doesn't need the posturing of a bullying tyrant here. Luca was in on the act - so Cadiz ushers him along with a smirk.

This speakeasy bar serves local rum and local women, but Cadiz seeks the rum. The Indian barman saw him come in and has already lined up cups of the latest brew to find its way to the port. Cadiz samples them while Luca shares a shot and a joke with the barman - the only other Indian left standing after a smallpox outbreak among their group of migrants.

Cadiz has a few private moments to reflect on his strange bond with Luca. Could he disclose the city of gold reputed to be north of Florida? King Carlos hopes to finance a new crusade on Jerusalem, so fame and fortune was promised to anybody who found such riches. He interrupts the laughter.

"What's funny Luca?"

"Captain, we joked about the pictures we are selling. I am being well paid for my scrolls of the bloodthirsty Indians." He spits on the floor, licks his lips, and curses.

Luca hasn't mastered the Spanish mannerism of spitting yet.

"Well done. We can add the three sixes of the devil later."

Cadiz takes a bottle with two cups, and sits down, kicking another chair out for Luca. Both are fully restored after their stormy return to the island. Luca had been boson to the Indian passengers while the real boson, Marco de Serena, was in the ship's cells. Now Luca wears smart Spanish clothes, and despite struggling with the boots, he can change from Chicoran brave to expedition interpreter as easily as a tossed piece of eight.

"Luca, you said that Indian queens worship the three sixes." Cadiz rolls his hands together. "If I cannot find gold, we can tell Columbus that they idolise the devil. Then he will tell the King and start a war. I know how to make a profit from that, but it took twenty-five years to defeat the Aztec. They eventually became a plague-ridden bunch of bandits, and I don't have that much time."

"Captain, you grew up in a peaceful Spain. What happened? How did the feuds begin, leading to raids and wars? What broke the trust built since the Moorish dynasties?" Luca has never touched the captain before, but breaks that taboo by leaning forward and taking him by the shoulders. The rum loosens his manners more quickly, as he has not spent a lifetime hardening his body to its effects. Luca's normally blank face then mimics a Spanish look of sympathy – a tilted head, sad eyes, and a glum mouth. "Fear is the key, but it will not spread easily. In our native legends, support always beats selfishness. That is how people rose above the beasts."

Cadiz muffles his voice. "There is the same message from our prophets... love will defeat greed." He slumps in his chair, and then the talk of Aztec wars reminds him about horses. He sits upright again. "We might have another ally. Spanish horses have swum ashore from shipwrecks for thirty years. If the Indians learn to ride, this will upset the agreed hunting-grounds, previously claimed on foot." He clenches his fists. "Bandits and raiders will have the advantage for the first time in your history. Hoarding and self-defence will sweep away any peace."

Luca copies the excitement. "I saw a print of devils on horseback in the library of Governor Toledo."

"The Four Horsemen of the Apocalypse, yes. They represent Pestilence, War, Famine and Death but how could we use them?"

"If Indian Cast-Outs use the spirits of the horse, then they might start the raiding you suggest."

Luca bows his head, and the eagerness he has copied from Cadiz suddenly ebbs away. At the phrase 'Cast-Outs', the rum invites something like sadness into Luca's mind. He reflects that he was himself a runaway, if not a true outcast. He pictures vaguely his family lined up at the edge of his village as he walked away into exile.

Cadiz doesn't notice Luca's change of mood, and charges on like a baited bull.

"Luca, you're a genius. I can sell weapons to all sides." He thumps the table. "When we find gold, I will be richer and more famous than Cortes."

The cups jump, some rum spills, and the bottle starts to fall… until Luca sweeps it back upright in a flash.

Cadiz twitches and fidgets, checking that the disturbance has not been noticed. He damns Dominica for being awash with spies, trading snippets of information about whether Florida is an island, or where a route to the west could be found. Cadiz knows that his own plans to explore new lands, or find a way to the other side of the world, must be kept secret.

Luca stares at him waiting for his next outburst, but Cadiz huffs as he searches his thoughts for safer territory to discuss. He smirks as he recalls the debt owed to him by his former boson, banished among the Indians, and he decides the meeting can be closed with a declaration of intent to settle old scores.

"Curse that boson, Marco de Serena. He stole my favourite knife, yet he claims the slave girl has it. Banishment isn't enough. He'll pay for taking it, or his family will pay back in Castile."

Luca scratches his feeble beard and pinches his jowls. He has noticed how the Spanish make grand oaths when they want to please their leaders.

"Captain Cadiz. That satanic slave girl will go up river, and she will find the Santee tribe in their spring settlements." He grips the crucifix around his neck. "I swear, in the name of God, I won't rest until I have killed the devil in her."

EMERALDS

A few nights after the bear attack, Inca fumbles with his knife by the river where the bear was slain. With the groan of the cascade filling his ears, and dried blood covering the pebbles, the knife seems to have a strange connection to the killing of the beast. His foreign father had left it during a visit from newcomers many seasons ago, and the emerald set in the scabbard fixes his eyes in an eagle's grip. Having taken his most potent drug for a séance with the bear, his trance compels him to chant to the spirits.

"Iney ichee ai oh. Iney ichee ai oh. Iney Iney Iney ah. Iney ichee ai oh."

Watching from nearby, Axa has also come back to absorb the spirit of the bear. To leave a kill without making peace with it can bring bad luck. Until soothed, this will haunt her, and afterwards she will be strengthened by the bravery of that great predator – but this boy got there first.

In the bright moonlight, the match between the boy's knife and her stolen knife startles her – though the etchings on the boy's knife have rope patterns compared to the zigzags on hers. The three-spiral carvings are slightly different but the jewels set in the scabbards are the same, and surely connected by their power.

Her mother's teachings about the meaning of the spirals come back to her.

'Trust prevails over the dark ages of survival at all costs, and we work together using our heads before our hearts.' Axa's mother could never have imagined that her princess might use these wisdoms in such a strange land.

A shiver runs down her spine at the pair of jewels, as

the boy seems to be from a far-off race in the northern oceans. Legends say they had high-priestess rituals before the evil horsemen came, and this knife may be their relic.

The angular design on her stolen knife is more like the Arab weapons, used by the same people that captured her and killed her family. How treacherous had been their offering of trade, followed by brutality! Spirits will curse forever the tribe that ransacked her village. They will fall apart, as the legends foretell the end of war-like people.

She returns to the present and forces herself to reason with it. Two different knives with the same jewels… truly the world is a joined-up place. Their journeys have been separated by the longest rivers and widest seas, and eventually the emeralds have found their way from their mine to this place. If these emeralds can be re-united, it will double their spiritual power.

She can join the boy in chanting for the bear and unite the jewels. This will make her irresistible to the red queen when he surely tells her. In the dreamy light, and in Inca's drunken state, it doesn't take much to catch his thoughts. Mimicking his song, she weaves her voice into his as she circles around him.

"Iney ichee ai oh. Iney ichee ai oh. Iney Iney Iney ah. Iney ichee ai oh."

With the hypnosis complete, she slides the Celtic knife from his grasp. Together they worship the Mother of Death, who passes them the spirit of the bear. Then she takes both knives, leaving behind both scabbards - before gliding away and releasing the spell. Now the far-travelled emeralds are next to each other on the boy's belt for the first time since they were mined in some far-off place and time.

When Inca comes around, he realises he has lost his knife but gained a new scabbard.

He dashes around, lifting pebbles and river-worn rocks to find the knife. Patting both the scabbards, and then pulling at his hair, he hopes he is still dreaming. How can this be?

Something killed the bear with a single slice.

His father's knife vanishes.

The emerald in his father's scabbard now has a sister, set in a new scabbard on his belt.

He runs back along the trail of dried blood from the bear and stubs his toe with a scream. This is no dream. This is a special day in the story of the Santee, when a visitor from another world has given him the sign of a new jewel.

Whichever goddess left it must control supernatural powers, and he will be taking a big risk by wearing it back to the village. Somehow, he must explain why he has two very important scabbards but not their knives.

GIFTS

Ona sits alone in her tepee, doodling spirals on her forehead with a piece of charcoal. She studies the two empty scabbards, with their spiral carvings talking to each other, and lessons from her mother spring from the back of her mind.

'Little Ona, there is harmony between the seasons and forces of nature.' She strokes the Three Spirals on her smock for reassurance. 'The spirals symbolise rebirth without upsetting the balance. Time and life itself have no beginning and no end, but happen over and over, round and round.'

The gift of a new emerald makes perfect sense. This is a sign of peace not war, even if it does mean the stranger has the actual blades. These are the workings of the Mother of the Gatherings whose benevolent spirit wants the two queens to meet as much as they do themselves.

Sitting among her blankets with their musty smells and textures, Ona inspects the pelt of the dead bear. The cleanness of the wound is still clear. The knife that made this cut is much better than Inca's. It may belong to this new scabbard, but what is the spiritual purpose of two empty scabbards... however beautiful and miraculously linked? The black queen must feel the same way about the two knives, even if they are more useful in their own right.

Warm light soaks through the skin of the tepee, warming Ona's heart. This first exchange of gifts hints at the start of a beautiful friendship. Perhaps the black queen has a playful sense of humour. Imagine what pranks they could play, and how much fun they might have when out scouting, away from their high-bound duties.

Reluctantly, she wipes the charcoal spirals from her brow and goes outside to face the gossip. As usual, the chirping and piping of birds mixes with the calling and gentle drumming of the scouts. Children play and the teenagers are sleeping-off their overnight adventures, but she can feel everyone else is on edge. Ona knows she has struggled to keep the adults calm... to explain away the black queen... and account for the death of the bear.

She sees Chet is nearby and the whole tribe are within earshot, sitting on their haunches and politely pretending to be busy with chores. She folds her legs on a mat, with Chet mirroring this a few moments later. By the power of some unseen force, the forest and livestock fall silent. The children warily follow suit and the rustling of Ona settling on the sheet of wicker is the only sound.

"Queen Ona, 'Morning Star' has a fine blade at her hand." Chet ventures with a wry smile. He has noticed the smudged spirals on her temples, but keeps it to himself.

"Chet, something closer to home has brought that knife." Ona returns the mockery. "We have never seen such a clean wound on any carcass and news of the spirals on the black queen's forehead is everywhere."

"Young Inca has a big mouth."

At this comment, a ripple of laughter spreads out among the gathered clan. Most of them are no longer hiding their eavesdropping, but looking towards their queen. Ona looks at the beads she flicks round her fingers and when she looks up, Chet and everybody else looks down.

"Take care Ona," Chet leans forward. "Even you may not be safe with such a hunter."

"I am the best hunter among the Santee women and

still ready for action - with breeding from the fittest and fastest princesses and the finest studs in the clans," she says, " ...but I may be a little rusty."

"I mean no offence," Chet drops his gaze again. "It is only that the other woman may have the luck of a better blade."

"She may have better contact with the gods." Ona invites more grovelling.

"No one has better contacts with the gods than you," he barks in horror at the thought.

"In that case I shall meet her, and meet her alone."

Chet falls into her trap and must now agree, or risk insulting his queen. He mumbles approval and everyone else quietly returns to everyday matters.

Ona returns to her tepee for some private thought. A meeting with the black queen is the best way to settle the community, but the next matter is how? Should she involve Inca? He is a terrible gossip and in the end, he is a runt. He has playful mystical powers but this is grave spiritual business. She could slip out of the camp and wait to be contacted - perhaps in a song.

Hopefully they will enjoy the royal friendship, but there is still a risk of mishap, or even murder. She is responsible for the health and happiness of her people and her daughters are not ready to succeed her.

In a nearby place, Axa has similar ideas. A meeting is a good idea but just thinking about it makes the devil spirits show in her mind. Alone and in hiding for much of the time, she finds a deep, abandoned cave but it is full of worrying ghosts. Lit by a small fire, she sees ancient paintings and carvings depicting small horses and beasts from another era. Only the proud Arab horses favoured by the Spanish roam the land now, so they must have come with that tribe. One new painting shows these new arrivals as a two-headed, four-legged creature - man and horse as one animal – and it is covered in warning symbols like the coyote thief.

She remembers stories about lands of a golden fleece where horses upset the balance. This led to a raiding, feudal world, but the Ashanti elders laughed this off as no more likely than camels causing warfare in the jungle.

Making herself snug, deep in the guts of this labyrinth, the only sound is the emptiness and the echo of her breathing. The glow of her small fire doesn't breach the blackness, but the dried spraints of ancient creatures form a spongy mattress.

Within the lair, images of half-human monsters fly around in the void. Curse these devils from the Atlantic crossing, but now she can test herself by facing them head on, with nothing to help her but the paintings left by the cave-dwellers from another time. This is her chance to confront the monsters and defeat them. Come evil spirits, come out of hell… .

The doors of the underworld don't open.

Perhaps they are afraid.

She allows herself to think of meeting with the queen again… Clan Mother, how could we meet?

"Here in hell." comes the reply from an image of the other queen, as soon as it shows.

Axa suddenly retches two or three times from a near-empty stomach. Spitting out the last of the acid in her mouth, she stares out again into the pitch-black canvas.

"What spirit is this…?" Axa yells, only to hear it echoing back, "…with three spirals on your horned head-dress. Half-woman, half-owl - come near me and I will kill you."

The owl-woman sweeps forward, talons bared and

screeching insults. "Ashanti assassin, I will kill you first."

Axa slashes at the spectre, trading insults until utterly spent, and falls onto her hands and knees praying... "Go back to hell. Please go back to hell. Please stop torturing me. Please, for the love my ancestors."

In her tepee, Ona senses something is wrong. A far-off but piercing soul is in panic, and it can only be the black queen. She turns her ears but there is no further word on the wind, just the chill of doubt.

A meeting may be a good idea - but it is very risky. The other choice is to do nothing. Wait, and let the black queen take the risks. In the meantime, she can try another gesture such as leaving the scabbards on a rocky outcrop. Power of love, this will show that talks are under way. If the black queen leaves the knives in the empty scabbards, this will be a sign to the Santee that she is a good queen. Hopefully, there will be no more surprises in store for them.

AMBUSH

After the usual ritual the next morning, Inca tells Ona about a fight during the night in the men's lodge. It's not surprising. The men normally respond to uncertainty with squabbling. She had seen their antics when every child's field-craft was proved by creeping up on the lodge and observing it in silence.

No doubt they still chant, dance, and get drunk... then fight with each other in old fancy dress, just as they have always done. They can have the secrecy they demand for the sake of the balance of forces in the tribe. The rites of the men hold no sway over Mother Earth and her moods, and any male status is only as fleeting as their often-shortened lives.

Other queens at the great gatherings hadn't had it so easy. They warned of places where wizards had risen up against witches, leading to havoc and the demise of those clans. Rumour has it, some tribes that live as nomads on the Great Plains had suffered this breakdown.

Few trust these stories, and there are no relics to back them up. In fact, the many objects swapped at the gatherings show the opposite, with queens talking peacefully - and even the most stubborn men wouldn't wish this tragedy for their tribe.

With news of this fight, Ona chooses to hasten the bonding with the black queen. Inca can leave the two empty scabbards for the mystery woman at the nearby site for burning the dead.

Fetching the scabbards, she notices a different knot in the ties at the back of her tepee and her plan is jolted forward. There is also the tell-tale sweeping of the dust when someone is covering their tracks. Is the baffling stranger in there or has she been and gone? There are no marks coming out.

It is best not to stop, and be heard to have noticed that something is different - so she enters the tent as if nothing is unusual. Both the scabbards now have their knives snugly in place. If the stranger intends to kill her, then it will be done before Ona's eyes have adjusted to the darkness inside.

The visitor is capable of murder - killing a bear proved that - but she should be a queen in her own right, and murder isn't the queen's way. The knife that killed the bear is surely the one in the new scabbard in front of her, so everything now depends on the spirit of the Three Spirals.

She waits for a lesser blade to sweep across her throat, but none comes.

Ona knows Queens do things in a different way, and not a single legend tells of murder for power. Since the Dreamtime, the Clan Mothers have ruled by marrying their children in careful diplomatic exchanges. Inter-breeding is good for their children's health and wit, but above all, it is good for the tribes. None of the paintings or carvings depicts brutality towards other clans, and none of the bones of the ancestors bear the scars.

Ona cannot even smell the stranger, never mind see her. There are a few furs and blankets with a small shrine for the Spanish helmet, and everything apart from the knives is just as she left it.

"I will cover my eyes and you can reveal yourself." She puts her palms on her face and kneels in the centre of the space.

Axa lowers herself soundlessly from above the entrance and kneels in front of the Clan Mother.

Ona's heart pounds at the thought of the first sight of the visitor. Only inches away, she still cannot catch her scent - not even in her breath. There is only the odour of her own furs and blankets, so she must have had time to smother herself in them.

Ona's nostrils flare and the hairs on her neck stand on end. Nothing in the most fertile undergrowth explains it. Not aniseed or mint. Not pepper or sage. What is that presence? Parting her hands like a child, Ona sees that the stranger's eyes before her are calmly closed in deference to Ona's rank. Three spirals are beautifully incised into the skin on her forehead, and they have all been done at the same time... at birth.

How youthful she is to be a fully-fledged queen.

In the time-honoured way, she gently takes the young woman's shoulders in her hands and tips her own head towards this high-ranking guest.

Axa tips forward and they touch noses. Gently moving her head back, Axa opens her black-brown eyes and smells the joy coursing through the Clan Mother's veins. She shivers from the power of the red queen's warm and wilful heart, before they embrace and laugh aloud.

SABOTAGE

"Inca, come pow-wow with me," Chet says, and they go to a nearby grotto pretending to set traps. Inca gets a piggyback and gets off into a tree as they get to their hiding-place. Chet stretches his great frame out on the mossy bed, while Inca slips down and perches next to him on a boulder. It was Chet's request, so he begins the pow-wow.

"Little friend, every love story causes jealousy. Your grandmother, Poco, is burning with envy about this black witch giving power to her younger sister Ona."

"Chet, I see this, but why does she feel it is unfair that Ona is our queen?"

"As you know, the royal line passes through daughters, who wear two spirals, and granddaughters, who wear one spiral. Poco had a daughter but no granddaughters, so she could not become queen. Her daughter's line ended with only you."

"So, I am her only grandchild - a misfit boy - while Ona's youngest daughter Jay has two fine girls, sired by you. This guarantees the Clan Mother's line for two more families." Inca dozes off, but mumbles for Chet to continue.

"You are right, little wizard. Signs like the black queen and the emeralds coming together across the lands also prove that Mother Fate has chosen Ona wisely. Poco's annoyance has led to her carving figurines of her fake granddaughters and she prays to them secretly at a shrine in her tepee."

Both of them wriggle into a more comfortable spot, and the pow-wow fades into dreams. In the cool, silent grotto, Inca mumbles to himself... "Jay my queen, Jay my queen."

Chet chuckles at Inca's fantasy. Of course, he hopes that his wife Jay will become Clan Mother in due course, but everything depends on all members of the clan eventually finding their rightful place - at least in this life. He replies, even though Inca's childish mind has wandered off to another world.

"We all have our part to play, my little friend. This is how the balance of nature works for all time. Feisty princesses aren't unusual, but Jay is a one-off. She is a spark that might start a forest fire. She's the one who will shake up the spirits, before settling them in a new balance."

Slowly, Chet too drifts off to sleep.

Back in the village, Poco's twisted heart turns every time she hears Ona and Axa laughing together. She wails privately to the figurines in her tepee, surrounded by the sounds of chinking stone statues and beaten metal ornaments, as she endlessly shuffles the symbols around.

"Now Ona harnesses the power of the black queen, the two emeralds, and the helmet she already has. Even Inca promises all his magic to her, but if I can turn Ona's daughters against her, justice might be found."

As teenagers, their mother had warned Poco and Ona about the burden of leadership.

"One of you must wear the Clan Mother's feathers, but they can weigh you down as well as help you fly," she had said in her final days.

"Dear sister Poco," the teenage Ona had later asked, "how can the feathers of the goose with its long flights weigh us down?"

"Ona, you silly girl," Poco had teased. "The feathers on our pottery and costumes are all signs of duty. As queen, I will have to bear this burden soon enough."

It was not to be.

She sees portrayals of herself in the landscape, drawn on rocks or carved on trees. 'Future queen falls from perch,' proclaims a picture of a two-spiral bird lying on its back. The logo of Poco is unmistakable. 'Your royal line is broken,' declares a carving of a Poco-bear, nurturing a coyote cub.

Praying at her shrine, she sees a chance. Can Ona's defiant nature be found in Jay and turned into jealousy? Evil Eye, their mother is in love with a new girl not even linked to the ancestors. Dear legends, she pleads to the Underworld, twist the spirits of trust that wear their hearts on their sleeves, making them so vulnerable.

Poco wrings her hands – the stubborn Jay is a good choice, and Ona had broken her heart last spring when she slept with Chet - the father of her daughters. Jay sometimes shaved her head and refused to wear Santee studs and earrings for several moons at a time, if she did not get her way.

There aren't yet any formal pictures of Jay in the landscape, Poco muses. Instead, there are many childish signs of worship carved by young boys who find her so captivating. One day, surely, there will be formal pictures of Jay revealing a gorgeous princess, with signs of gutsy and wayward instincts... motifs like the snake and the lightening.

JUSTICE

Ona and Axa share objects, drawings, and songs - chatting with ornate signs as they swap legends and ideas. Axa talks of her childhood and Ashanti puberty rituals, but cannot bring herself to say what terror brought her to this land.

"Tell me when you are ready," Ona would say, as she noticed Axa's dry mouth, or cold hands.

The days and the moons slip by and Mother Fate weaves her web around the Santee tribe, having brought a new green jewel and a sister queen. Axa regrows her hair into beaded plaits and loves the lines of spots painted on her face and body by the children.

The air smells of Spring at last, and the evening is particularly calm as the campfires splutter and the wolf-chorus dies down with the sun. Only Ona notices that the chorus is slightly closer and a little more fretful.

"The wolves normally obey the truce with people," Ona says to Axa, "but even more grudgingly than the bear. The late spring makes the big predators struggle for survival and I have no power to pow-wow with a pack of hungry wolves."

A known macho shouting shatters the peace, and an unknown, wretched begging.

"Here's a curse on your soul," Chet booms.

"Have mercy on me, have mercy on me," a far-off tongue replies.

Chet has captured a scruffy stranger stealing grain, and they emerge from the trail that leads through the forest to the huts holding the harvest. The dust of years of trodden leaves billows as Chet walks, but it barely makes a sound under his rolling gait.

Incredibly strong, he clutches the bedraggled man

easily in one hand, while waving a strange object in the other.

"Typical Chet," Ona whispers to Axa. "In the nearby mountains there's a doorway of standing stones, with a huge plinth that was put there by the ancestors. To become a man a boy must walk through, and when his arms touch the sides, he is ready. Even before the hair grew under his arms, Chet was so big and strong that he was able to carry the plinth away on his shoulders."

"Where did you get this metal pipe?" Chet demands, holding the stranger up like a rag-doll. "Weasels have no use for smoking pipes."

He has taken the stranger's pistol for a trophy, but Ona recognises it straight away as the same kind of object they buried with the ashes of the honoured Celtic and Spanish visitors, so many seasons ago. No one ever guessed what it was for, apart from perhaps smoking tobacco. The noblemen never said, before they died of sickness. She briefly dreams of their visit when she was a youth, and how amazing their stories were, until the gods chose to take them beyond the abyss.

Despite his poor state, Axa knows the thief is Marco, the sailor who let her go, but she says nothing. Weeks as a prisoner and weeks in the forest haven't served him well, and this once sturdy boson has become a starving wreck of a man.

He knows Axa of course, but also chooses to see what awaits him.

Ona knows there is only one fate in the Santee way. For openhearted and unarmed visitors there is always a welcome and honour, but for thieving or lies - the sentence is death. Nearby, an outcrop of rocks is set aside for such things, but it has never been used since everyone knows the rules. There are plenty of stories of death sentences, which have the effect of deterring grave wrongdoing and lies.

Stories of mercy and banishment also abound, but custom regards such shame as even worse than death. There are some stories of deals being made, where a reason can be found to allow mercy.

Ona rushes around the folklore, to find a reason to pardon this poor man, but the tribe expects her to uphold the law.

Her dear Mother didn't teach this other than in childish acting. What should Ona do? When it was child's play, it was easy… 'Death to the thief,' she would declare… but what should she do with a real thief, and everyone staring openly. In the play-acting, her mother sometimes found reasons to spare the errant soul. Ona begs silently for ideas regarding this feeble man.

She couldn't even remember the ritual for putting someone to death, but goes ahead declaring, "Axa, Chet, and I will take the thief to the prayer sticks."

"Ritual states that I, Poco, and Princess Jay, must also attend as witnesses," Poco announces to the group.

"There's no need for witnesses at a death sentence, but you may come." Ona reluctantly agrees, sensing that it will be more troublesome to stop her.

They all stride off to the sacrificial site, dragging Marco and leaving the rest of the village in shock. Nobody will enjoy this barbaric act, not even Chet, but the myths state that the spirits of justice need a soul, or lawlessness will consume their people. It had to be done and quickly. Axa fetches the two ceremonial knives, but her dithering suggests she will be reluctant to use them on this particular throat.

Mother's love, Ona prays, come now and give a reason to pardon this man. He's not even from this land

and his feeble body needs bread. Her long dead, much-loved mother doesn't show in her mind's eye and no ominous eagle or owl is heard. No snake or spider slithers or scampers across the track. Finally, at the sacrifice site, Ona's training overcomes her doubts.

"Axa will kill the kneeling thief with the new knife," she demands, as soon as they get to the hallowed place. Delicately painted prayer-sticks are planted in the ground surrounding the outcrop, with feathers to catch the wind. The clearing hosts a spring show of grasses, shrubs and hemlock. This is a beautiful place to die, and be born again in another form.

Frantically, Axa gestures that she wants the thief spared, at least from her blade. He helped her escape from the ship - so the gods will not accept ruthless revenge. She never told the full story of her own captivity and now in the heat of the moment, she cannot find the language or signs to explain this.

"Not me Ona, please ask the others, or let him go."

Guiding Light, is this your sign? No one has defied Ona since she became queen, but a surge of energy doesn't guide her to mercy or anger. Execute him and be feared forever as a ruthless leader, or pardon him and risk chaos.

Poco saw that Marco and Axa knew each other and had planted a figurine in his pocket before the group left the village. She had readily picked it up from her group of carvings at the shrine in her tepee, and she told Jay her plan on the way to the site. Axa's pleading for mercy plays into her trap.

"Jay it's time," Poco whispers. "Tell them of your dream, and don't forget the little statue."

"Ona wait." Jay shrieks. "I had a dream of Axa breast-feeding a daughter while the father was fetching a blanket. That father was this thief."

Jay rushes to the quivering stranger and produces the figurine from his pocket, to prove her claim, before continuing.

"Ona, in the dream I saw Axa give him a little statue of their daughter marked with spirals, to remind him of their bond."

Ona's crude rage burns at the evidence of a plot to usurp her, but the figure shows a two-spiral princess. Grabbing it, her wariness takes over, knowing the Ashanti use three spirals from birth and have no two-spiral princesses. All-Seeing Eye, this cannot be Axa's tribute to this man.

Everybody looks to the Queen of the Santee, but a rustling in the undergrowth at the edge of the clearing catches Ona's attention.

"My queen, my queen." Inca emerges from the forest wearing the Spanish helmet.

His puny neck can hardly hold his head up straight.

Marco sees his family motif on the helmet and frantically points to the pistol in Chet's hand – also marked with the family crest.

With everybody stunned by Inca, Axa pulls herself together first and snatches the pistol and helmet, before laying them on the ground in front of Ona. Everyone can see the matching symbols on the two shiny, foreign objects.

Ona stuns the group by declaring, "Poco and Jay, you two are spiders."

COINCIDENCE

Ona lifts her chin and canvasses this site intended for sacrifice. This nest of rocks enjoys all the splendour of the Appalachi Mountains, wrapping the Santee in a blanket of natural wealth. Stunted oak and hickory forests surround them, and spruce fir gives the horizon its blue-green hue. It's a beautiful setting for brutal acts. She silently blesses her ancestor. 'Mother, thank you for showing me how to lift the death sentence on this pathetic figure. Wherever he came from, he can return there knowing our mercy.'

"Jay's dream is a fraud," she announces, "Axa's people mark the three spirals at birth, so this figurine cannot be Ashanti. This little statue only proves that Poco, and now my own Jay, are possessed with envy. I will not have that shape-shifting ghost among my people."

She swallows her anger.

"This thief is related to our most honoured trophy. The symbol on his pipe speaks to the symbol on that helmet, and I will spare him for this reason."

She grabs him and Axa by the hands and joins them in a formal kinship – before presenting them with the two emerald-embedded scabbards.

"I hereby declare these two newcomers to be sister and brother. The emeralds symbolise their two worlds coming together in our land."

With a further flourish, she makes several decrees. "Poco, you are banished from tribal rituals." Then she turns to Jay and Chet. "Jay, you are young and will be pardoned for your part in this plot to shame Axa. You and Chet must forget your petty feud. My feelings for him are in the past, but yours are in the future."

Everyone sighs with relief at the end of this grand speech, other than Axa. Her mind has switched to other hunters. About twenty-five hungry wolves now encircle them. Ona had warned Axa about their pack mentality and their frantic eating habits.

As the circling, demented pack closes in, the colour drains from the faces of the sacrificial group. Skin gets clammy, they feel sick, and blood rushes from their guts to fill their muscles and sharpen their senses instead. The rest of the village are a hand-of-time away, and they will not get there before the frenzy of wolfing human flesh begins.

Out of the blue, Jay, Poco, and the faithful Inca offer themselves in sacrifice.

"I can feed the wolves." Jay exclaims in denial of her shame.

"I too," Inca yells, raising himself as high as he can, with heartfelt duty to the clan cause.

"I too," Poco mumbles.

"Run for the village," Jay orders the others.

"Inca there's nothing on you to eat," Chet declares, "make yourself useful and start a fire."

Nevertheless, the three would be martyrs begin a sacrificial chant. They hold hands together towards the sky, turning their backs to the wolf pack closely surrounding them. With fiery glances, the others and even Marco, refuse the offer of escape.

Instead, they form a circle facing the wolves head on. Ona, Axa, and Chet draw their knives and go into their own survival trance. With crystal clarity they visualise the first wolves leaping at their throats, teeth bared. Those wolves will get their best blades.

They have other knives strapped to their legs and can roll away slashing at throats and eyes. Axa also has her three-pronged stabbing weapon and she checks its place at the small of her back. It might be useful in her death throes.

Limbs are charged and ready to release lightning, writhing as the bloody veil falls over their gaze. In this infernal state, they can ignore the first bites. Blood will shy away from wounds, while their blades take their toll. At least the braver wolves will die with them.

The barking and snarling turns to low growls of intent, and the foremost wolf sprints forward, leaping at Ona. Jay turns round and fires her first arrow into its open mouth. Ona steps aside and Inca smashes the helmet onto its already lifeless skull as it lands in a heap.

Several other wolves run and jump at their first targets - Chet, Axa and Marco. Chet sidesteps and smashes his club into the mouth of one, while Axa ducks and pins the jaws of another together with an upward sweep of her knife.

Jay arrows the wolf heading for Marco between the eyes, but more wolves are right behind the first wave and going for the legs and arms of the warriors.

Ona, Axa and Chet each manage to stab the second wave of wolves in the neck, but the other wolves slavering jaws are already finding human skin and bone.

Marco fumbles around for his gunpowder, raises his pistol to the sky and fires a shot. The shock wave rings out across the wilderness and echoes from the mountains that have never heard such a sound before.

MUTANT

Instantly the wolves start squealing and rolling around as if the sound has scrambled their brains. Dazed and in panic, the wolf pack are easily split up and chased off. Jay puts three more arrows in different wolves as they retreat, before Ona tells her to stop. Among the warriors, saliva from the wolves mixes with human blood that is trickling from several gashes and puncture wounds. They all fall to their knees shaking and check for further danger.

Poco had not attempted to fight, but starts collecting nettles to wipe the wounds, while all the villagers and every scout in the valley are running towards the crack of exploding gunpowder - to protect their queen. Their callings can be heard from every trail, and Ona knows that nothing will ever be the same again. She squats next to the broken skull of the first wolf to attack, and she strokes its mane as one monarch to another. The other warriors limp into place around her, and Inca finishes off some severely injured wolves using the swinging helmet as a club.

Ona, the Queen of the Santee, gathers her thoughts to the rising sound of rescuers, the fading sound of dying wolves, and the settling of the warrior's breathing. She looks towards the far-off blue ridge and wonders if she is dreaming. While the gods and devils fight over the explosive new force, the shock-wave will echo as far as the abyss in the west. Is it the sound of the Middleworld tearing apart? Ona must be calm and use this newcomer with the pistol to help settle the clans.

*

As village life gets back to normal, the work of growing and storing food for the winter leaves Ona little time to reflect. Nevertheless, something has changed forever. Is a force from another place climbing up from the Underworld? Powers of balance, even the Overworld may not be able to control such energy.

Marco gradually picks up the language and the signs, and he shows a talent for acting and drawing. At a meeting about grain sharing, he is invited to talk about the Spanish tribe. The arching willow-framed hut whispers, rather than hums like a tepee, while sunshine peeks through the wicker walls. There are no personal belongings and it feels business-like and purposeful.

"Ona," Marco explains, "my voyage took the rest of the Africans back to their island stronghold in the Caribbean, before any settlement was built."

He looks at Axa, too late to withdraw his comment about aborting the voyage, but she stares into the middle distance. Now she must feel even further from her homeland, but at least he too is banished and abandoned. He keeps Axa's captivity a well-guarded secret and, as far as he can tell, no one talks about the marks on her wrists and ankles from the chains. Maybe, like him, she feels a mixture of shame and denial about her trauma.

"Marco," Ona says, "there have been more sightings of ships out to sea. In recent moons, scouts have seen three vessels at the mouth of the Santee River itself. Curse or blessing, one has foundered on a sandbank as a sign that the Spanish are trying to find an anchorage again."

Marco absorbs these facts before a nod from Ona allows him to speculate.

"Governor Juan Toledo will be erecting stone markers to claim the lands north of the island of

Dominica. I know that about ten summers ago, a captain called Miruelo explored the west coast of this place they call Florida, and a captain called Cordova landed on the western shore. He was surprised and put off by a large group of the Appalachi, but the Spanish will be back in ever-greater numbers... it is just a matter of where and when."

In the nights after this meeting, Ona cannot sleep, and finally wakes Axa rather than face the dawn alone. She sings a lullaby until Axa stirs, before gently stroking her forehead.

"What is it?" Axa mumbles.

"Nothing."

"Even in my sleep I could hear you turning. Is it the sailors?"

"Perhaps. I need to imagine what the sailor tribe can offer, or whether they are only a threat."

Axa sits up and strokes Ona's forehead, but the skin is clammy, and loose.

"Ona, you have not been right for a day or two, we need to speak to the medicine women. Forget the sailors, or they will eat at your soul before they even come ashore."

"Darling Axa, I have got a fever, but there is something else that never features in the legends." She shows Axa some red sores in her mouth.

"My queen, we will wake the witches straight away."

In the next few days, Ona finds her limbs heavy and her thoughts waxy. She confines herself to her tepee but Marco persuades the medicine women that he can leech out some of the illness and becomes a devoted nurse to Ona. At the height of the disease, the Santee queen feels her skin lifted into pockmarked warts all over her body.

Every part of her becomes a muddled crowd of spongy, coral-like swellings jostling cheek by jowl, completely concealing the beauty beneath. Marco politely refuses her request for a polished shell to see her face. Only her eyes are spared the fearsome mutant she has become - and she knows this too well from her shaking, encrusted fingers exploring her features... she doesn't need to see it as well.

She can only pray... demons from the Underworld, stay in your place! Has that gunshot released your monsters? Ona will not let you any further. Turn this Santee queen into a fungus if you must, but don't try to reach the Overworld. This monarch is still a Three Spiral shield from your evil. All the animals and plants of the Middleworld will be born again here on Earth – in paradise. None will let you pass. None will help you climb towards the sky.

After the worst of the fever, Ona feels her skin recover slowly, but her eyesight is scarred and she clearly won't be well enough to represent the Santee at the tribal gatherings this autumn.

"Gatherings are the oldest part of our culture," she explains to Marco, remembering the legend that a newcomer could save her people from hell, "Power of the clans, this time the Santee group will be Axa, my beloved twin daughters, and you Marco."

Marco listens patiently, putting his hand over his mouth to conceal his surprise as Ona continues.

"My twins, Nani and Nana, have only had a son and a stillborn daughter between them, though there is still time for them to have girls. They are older and better known to the other queens, but as the seasons have gone by it is Jay's motherhood of two girls by Chet that promises a new royal line. Anyway... gatherings."

He raises his eyebrows.

"My dear Marco, let me draw it in the sand for you. I don't need my eyes for this, as it is quite simple."

She takes a stick and draws a handful of circles on the floor, then repeats this drawing off to the side of the first.

"These first five circles are the tribes of the Appalachi region in the east, including the Santee. This muster sends one tribal group to the Grand Council - represented by these second five circles. Here each circle now represents another region, north, south, central and so on. The royal families are so interwoven that everyone feels well represented."

"Is this how the taxes are gathered?"

"What are taxes?"

"Er… they are payments, or offerings… for safety."

Ona laughs. "You have so much to learn. We make gifts, building trust and love. Forget your primitive fears, we are shielded by our need for each other."

"My queen," Marco says, "your strength has recovered and so will your sight. You should go."

"My eyes will recover but the twins need to learn how to lead. I have decreed that Axa is care-taker queen until they have enough know-how."

"I know you have already sent scouts to tell the other queens that you will miss the event this year."

"Marco, that is the one thing I will miss. These days, gatherings are mainly for the traders, for the teenagers to flirt, and for royal matchmaking. For the elders like me, it is only the get-togethers at the private queen's lodge that make it worth going. We gossip about the old days and the hunting together. I can't tell you what we got up to."

CHESS

A doting group of youngsters surround Marco, listening to his tales of Saxon queens in the far-off past, and Queen Regents more recently in his part of the world. Other children gather round, playing games for testing memory and nimbleness, with the sounds of clashing pieces, cheers at victory, or wailing at defeat.

He has helped the Santee artists make a chess set, with each piece and each square decorated using tiny, flint drills. Bishops are now wizards, castles are burial mounds, and pawns are half-human, half-insect.

"See how the chess queen replaced the male chancellor, as the most powerful piece in the game," he asserted to Ona in one match.

Scouts are spreading his standing among all the tribes, but Ona says some of the more widespread tribes are starting to doubt the leadership of their Clan Mothers.

This morning he plays a game of chess with Jay, and he notes her runaway mind. They sit cross-legged in one of the gaming circles, surrounded by staring children.

"This time Marco," Jay begins, "I will re-use your captured pieces on my side."

"You cannot do that. When they are captured, they die. They are out of the game."

"How stupid. Life is a cycle."

A short silence grips the children, while Jay considers her next move. Eventually an ash seed circles gently down onto the board, breaking the spell.

Jay finally makes her move with the gusto of a ranting wizard at the lodge.

"So," she asks, "what would the chess queen do about wizards talking behind their backs and spreading fear?"

She looks straight at him and his heart jumps - he had forgotten how dangerous her green eyes were.

"Princess, fear isn't part of the game, but its ghost is like a genie out of a bottle... a phoenix out of the fire." He chooses his sayings from Arab and Greek myths, but the point isn't lost on the two-spiral princess.

"Marco, wizards see a link between fear, safety, and power, but queens know that once fear takes hold, it will feed on tolerance. Small signs of fear - like body-guards, weapons, and emblems of rank - will spread like a plague among the men."

"You are right," he says, making his moves slowly and methodically. "Your system of sharing will be replaced by hoarding, racketeering, and then fighting."

"Ona talks of a greedy, brutal, faithless cycle - until nature is crushed and all people are wiped out. Only the oneness of the Three Spiral queens can protect us from this havoc."

Marco laughs. "I suppose it is only a few missed meals that stand between any nation and anarchy."

His mind comes back to the chess but she sweeps up her horse and dashes it down.

"Checkmate."

He surveys the board for choices, but those piercing eyes had run him through, and he missed the mating move completely.

"Princess Jay of the Santee," he announces, "you win."

"I will be your queen soon enough. Now tell me how you came to the Santee. There were no signs, other than Axa coming on the wind. Why would the spirits send an African queen on the same wind as a thief, I mean tramp... er..."

"Or adventurer? I am a young man, whatever my

tribe. I followed Axa from the other side of the world, hoping her luck would be my fortune."

"What is 'fortune'?"

"It is hard to explain. In my old tribe, we value gold and great buildings. They are the symbols of our status and give us power," he adds sheepishly.

"Worthless objects give you power," she shakes her head.

Axa quietly watches Marco's chess match with Jay. What purpose awaits she and Marco – both newcomers - at the gathering? Ona has made her the caretaker queen, but what if her demons poison her mind? If Ona is right, the spirals will guide the outcome... if she is wrong, then the spirals may die with the dreams of peace.

Either way the shooting stars in the northern sky announce that it is time for the yearly pilgrimage. Together with the dogs and horses, and the usual cordon of scouts, they prepare to depart for the Alabama foothills.

Just before setting off, Axa finds Ona alone in her tepee and she asks her about the customs with the horses and other tribes. This animal offers chances to move faster, but surprises villages that aren't used to them.

"Axa my dear, there are some things I cannot teach you. Horses appeared in my mother's time. I have seen them spread among the tribes, but... like anything new... our culture is taking time to get used to them."

"I see they pull sleds, but are seldom ridden and never galloped."

"I can imagine a day when we will gallop them while hunting, but for now the bison are plentiful and the winter brings them to us. Our network of scouts can pass messages by drum or song... running to each other if necessary with gifts or pictures. Each clan can harvest its own territory on foot and we are rarely in a hurry, so horses are still a novelty."

"I see it is customary to cast out badly-behaved boys and sometimes girls. What if they used horses to raid the settlements?"

"Great Eagle forbid. Cast-Outs who don't submit would be hounded to the end of the world. They grovel to a new clan or tribe until they are accepted again, or they live out their lives alone."

"Could they join together and become a threat?"

"Dear Axa, you have some strange fears. The reason they become Cast-Outs is that they cannot come together like normal people. Anyway, it is time for you to go to your first gathering... as queen regent, no less."

Outside, a build-up of whooping, barking and neighing now fills the air. Dust is stamped into clouds of eagerness, and the parting is blessed with chants and hugs for all the porters and scouts.

Ona cannot bear to be there as the village sees them off, but Jay and Chet stay at her side and they all pray for a peaceful journey.

VISITORS

"Chet, are you awake? That mare in foal... I think she's given birth," Jay says.

He grunts and rolls over among the furs and blankets, while she wriggles away and sits in a ball. Her hair is plaited and tied, and a pot of unwanted jewellery sits nearby. Her dots of royal make-up are faded, making perfect cover. Through the smoke-flap of the tepee, the sky is strident with stars, so she winks one eye closed - saving it to survey the blackness of her home in a moment.

With the open eye, she cannot resist the Milky Way above, until a stiffening neck forces her back to the morning habits.

She swaps eyes open. Everything is as it was when she fell asleep - the clothes, the shrine, and the weapons. The moonlight shows the two spirals painted on the skins at the entrance. The other silhouetted symbols of the Sky Snake and the All-Seeing Eye look in on her too.

That's what woke her. It is time.

The Eye is exactly in line with the full moon. These are the simple lines that always watch her carefully, lifting her spirit to another place - to the Overworld. They symbolise a living being, talking with her soul, and giving her a feeling as certain as death. That's why the Sky Snake is also painted on her tepee, and why she will one day have the three spirals. Grabbing her weapons, she crawls out and stands upright. First doffing her head to the west - where the after-life waits beyond the Middleworld – then turning to face east.

Flexing her feet in the sand, the leather clothes rest on her hips and shoulders where they know her well. The bow and quiver slip across her body and the extra knife glides into the scabbard on her lower leg.

She holds her main knife over the moon and listens to the village sleeping - the snoring of the men, some babies on the breast, and slow-cooked pumpkin on the embers. The dogs are quiet and the whining of the mare has stopped. It must have been a dream.

Now she can focus on the wandering points of light in the night sky - the new visitors in this cycle of the moon. A string of starry beads is stretched just above the steaming forest in a manner rarely seen, and they do not circle the north star every night like normal stars. These are portents.

Queen Ona joins her, moving like a ghost because of her blindness.

"Princess, what do you see?"

"The arrival of the Spanish has brought this omen. The first visiting star represents their horses, spreading across the land. The next after the Morning Star is the sign of your sickness. The next is Axa... but it is the last of these, beyond the moon, that leads me away to the south. It is the star of Fear. You know the men are talking of having their own 'Great Gathering'."

"The men cannot arrange a village gathering without fighting, so nothing will change. The Three Spirals will overcome any fear."

Jay huffs before making her point. "That was true before the Spanish came. It has been true since the Dreamtime when the Breath Giver brought the rocks to life... but the sailors are from the Underworld." She pauses for a gut-wrenching moment. "It was the All-Seeing Eye that woke me this morning."

Ona shivers all the way down to the cold ground. The timing of this omen is strange - with the other Princesses so recently away to the queen's gathering. Jay lifts her chin and holds Ona's hand.

"Mother, even with the others away... perhaps because they are away... I must go south."

The two women are no longer alone. A small group of children are also pointing at the string of seasonal stars on the eastern horizon. They draw them in the sand on their map of the known patterns.

The early light soaks in from the Overworld as the forest breathes out. One of the boys grabs the stick from an older girl and it breaks. She beats him with her half and he makes a run for it, but he doesn't get far. Another girl stretches out a leg and trips him before they all give him a beating in the sand. They slap their moccasins wherever they can cause most hurt, but the boy doesn't cry.

"That's enough." Jay shouts into the lifting gloom.

It is impossible to see who started the quarrel. The fighting stops and the shamed boy runs off, after one final whack across the legs from the girl with the broken stick.

"Jay, you are only twenty summers, but one of your daughters is already the schoolteacher."

"Was that Kimi? Good for her, but even I could not see their faces."

"When your eyes let you down, you rely on other senses. I can assure you that was your own princess. She has your way with men."

"Mother that is unkind. You know as well as I do that boys only understand the carrot or the stick."

"Wise words, young thing... if you want them to move. What if you want them to stop? In fact you want them to do nothing." Ona eases Jay round to the subject of her quest to stop conflict with the sailor tribes.

"Do not try to stop me mother. You went on your walkabout at my age. You know it is my rite of passage, if I am to take over when you die. My older sisters may have a healthy boy, but boys don't continue the line."

"I'm not standing in your way. I just worry about your quest. My first journey was north, to ask the Inuit about the new ice age, then south to ask about the Taino of the southern islands. Breath Giver, how I wish I hadn't learned of their fate. Your journey will also be south, but about what matter?"

"The Spanish."

"Yes, but what about them? Many moons ago they came to the mouth of the Santee River… and they left. More recently, they left a ship on a sandbank. They will come and they will go. They left Axa, who makes us richer."

"They also bring horses, sickness and fear. The signs say I must go, and Chet can stay until you are fully recovered."

"Jay my love, the queens are away from their tribes at the gathering, and you will be without scouts or drums — so he must go with you. That is my final word."

"If you insist. The gathering of queens is in the west, but the stars send me south. That is my path until I know what the All-Seeing Eye has seen."

PROTECTION

Jay goes back to her tepee, just as Chet's son by another union skulks away wrapped in a blanket.

"Jay, my son has told me about a beating on the orders of our daughter... his own half-sister. He admitted he broke the prayer stick, but it was an accident."

"The prayer stick. That is bad... and he is having too many accidents these days. Perhaps if he wants to take such risks he should do it playing with the boys. You too went through this phase. He will be broken-in soon."

"He isn't a horse, he is a boy."

"And he will soon be a man. What kind of man do you want your son to be?"

"I want him to learn reason, not brutality."

"Consequences come first, before reason. When a boy understands consequences you can reason with him."

"Princess, thank the gods for our two girls, but we haven't had the blessing of a son. Perhaps we should ask Ona about this."

"I agree. Sorry Chet, but right now I have important things on my mind. The All-Seeing Eye woke me this morning. The stars that move very slowly around the Overworld are telling me to go south. Ona has decreed that you must come with me, but otherwise we travel fast and without scouts or drums."

Within a few days, they are paddling across the Savannah River. It's a well-used crossing and there are numerous canoes left on both sides of the broad meander.

"Chet, do you smell horses?"

"No Princess, but we are being watched."

"If you call me Princess again, then you will be sleeping alone tonight. There. Either side of the beach up ahead. Two horses and riders, but I can't see their tribe."

Chet skews the kayak with a single, powerful stroke.

"Jay, your nose is keener than my eyes. I think they may be Cast-Outs, but they look like braves from the Calusa clans who live south of the Santee River. This is a long way from the coast for those swamp people."

They paddle on as if nothing was unusual, and soon Chet is heaving their canoe onto the sandy shelf. Jay sees them break cover first. From either side of the beach, the boy and girl approach on their horses at an unruly trot. Neither has tribal feathers and they have empty holes around their ears, nose and eyebrows where their tribal symbols would normally be worn.

It crosses Jay's mind how much easier it would be to kill them on horseback. An arrow to the heart would go under the breastbone and skewer its target. While an arrow to the throat would go up into the brain. Death would be instant, instead of the choking of a normal neck-shot. Perhaps she could kill them both at the same time with her favourite trick – two arrows at a time.

"Whoah," the girl shouts, as they converge with the horses barely under control. Chet drops the canoe and whispers to Jay.

"I don't know if I should laugh or cry."

He steps forward and settles both the horses.

"Greetings." Jay loosens her shoulders. "Are you going to get down and share biscuits with us?"

Chet can see that her tolerance of surly teenagers is already stretched to its limit. He speaks to the girl, while the boy averts his gaze.

"Young lady, these are fine horses. Where did you find them?"

She doesn't reply, but the boy does. "Sir, one is from the shipwreck and one from the settlement."

Settlement? Shipwrecks are common but there are no stories of Spanish settlements. The boy then looks Chet in the eye for the first time.

"Sir, you can see we are Cast-Outs. If you want to know more, then you should take us in." He looks away again. Jay steps forward and holds out her palms.

"I am Princess Jay of the Santee and this is Chet. Do you have names?" The girl gets down, and is felled by her horse as it steps sideways. Chet puts out a hand to help her up, but she blushes, ignores it, and gets herself up.

"I am Free Bird. We have no tribe but we look after this crossing."

Jay folds her arms. Cast-Outs do sometimes try to live outside tribal groups, but they usually mind their own business. Sometimes they even form new tribes in new hunting grounds. Jay addresses her as if she had her own tribe already.

"Free Bird, we are on a Walkabout. The All-Seeing Eye has sent us here to your crossing. Perhaps you can look after it for our Santee tribe. Of course you will need to observe our customs and wear our symbols with pride."

"Princess Jay, you don't observe the customs of the Walkabout. You have no scouts and no drums."

Jay sees this girl is clever, and has surely been cast out for being too pushy - while the boy is hasty and afraid. All this is too much to deal with right now, so she comes to the point. "Tell us about the settlement, and we will share our finest meats before we go on our way."

The boy proudly gives up all he knows, flashing his fingers and clapping his hands together. "I counted ten hands of horses and sixty hands of settlers. Black people are cutting trees and making houses near the mouth of this river. The Kristianos give us trinkets if we worship their cross."

"That's enough." Free Bird slaps his horse and he goes back into his shell with a grunt. Jay sees her chance of finding vital facts.

"Free Bird please, why are the coastal tribes keeping this news to themselves?"

"Princess Jay of the Santee, this boy is dreaming. He has had too much cedar-bark tea. Now what about your safety? We can make sure you have safe passage in exchange for some beads and spices."

Chet sees Jay about to explode with anger, so he kneels next to Free Bird and produces some biscuits from his pouch.

"Free Bird, I thank you for your offer of safety - from Cast-Outs I assume. Here are some of our finest travel foods. Please accept our thanks and we will be on our way."

Free Bird takes the offering and Chet gives Jay a wink. He smiles and flicks his head for her to take a piggyback, since many clans from the swamps carry their leaders this way. She duly jumps onto his back and playfully smacks his rump.

"You see," Jay accepts the ride along the trail, "This Spanish settlement is the reason I was woken by the All-Seeing Eye ."

PART TWO

IMPACT

GATHERING

After travelling west for half a cycle of the moon, the Santee group gets to the valley of the gathering. Tribal chants fill the air and they greet some other tribes this way. Axa and the twins set up their tepee near to Marco and the male scouts, binding their new homes to the earth with more rituals.

As caretaker queen, Axa tries to reassure the twins about their role. Ashanti gatherings were so similar, and she knew those well. The dusk music of the forest animals is settling down as she speaks.

"Nani, Nana, eat and drink well, and then we will rest. Ona says there's much custom and ritual to get through."

"Aunt... I mean Axa. You are ignoring the young men that have come to our camp already," Nani grins. "They ride and run around, passing messages and doing chores, but they haven't been chosen by chance. Even you must have noticed the fine Wichita boys."

Nana couldn't resist joining in. "Aunt Axa, that Wichita errand boy has a smile like a row of elk teeth. Even Chet would want such a grin."

The princesses are about to launch into one of their frantic and witty exchanges, when Axa cuts them off. She loves them like sisters but she is too tired for a squabble.

"You need to think with your heads and not with your hearts." She stops when she sees the look of doubt on their faces - gatherings are about matchmaking, just as much as duty. "At least until the corn dance, " she adds shaking her head.

"Until the corn dance," the twins cry out together.

Both the Pensacola hosts and the neighbouring Wichita tribe had made proposals in the months beforehand. Several earlier visits to the Santee villages had allowed glances to be exchanged and flirting to take place. Axa and the princesses are expected to meet the princes who have been picked for them to choose from.

It gives Axa a reason to see her chosen match - Prince Kuruk of the Pensacola. He is tall and broad, but slim like the Masai from the grassy plains of Africa. He walks like a stag with faithful brown eyes, and he forced himself into her heart on his visit to the Santee a few months ago. 'Stop tipping your head when you look at me,' she had thought as he had gazed like a giant puppy seeing right through her.

She had sent a message for Kuruk to show her around, and they meet at the muster chambers - but find them full of other courting couples. They greet each other formally, and then quietly watch the twin princesses for a short time as they occupy another chamber with some Wichita boys. She slips back to her tepee ahead of the twins, musing about Kuruk. They would have time to meet more privately, and don't need to rush things.

Later that first night, Axa, Nani, and Nana get ready for sleep on the bed of furs in their tepee. The fire flickers its last flame, turning to purple and pink waves swimming among the embers.

Nani is restless. "Sister, come closer. I am feeling cold," she groans.

Does Nani mean for Axa to move closer? They are nearer in age than she is to their mother.

"You come here. I am feeling cold," Nana mumbles from the other side of the small space. They are like two sides of the same brooch. As the face of the jewellery, Nani is ornate and speaks in symbols and riddles. Like the back of a brooch, Nana is strong and practical.

"Little sister Nana, the cup should hold the acorn,

not the other way around," Nani insists. She was born first by a hand-of-time, and never lets Nana forget it.

"Nani, you can warm yourself up by coming here, and then I will be your cup as you wish," Nana chuckles.

"Rest my bones," Axa interrupts, "both of you come here and keep me warm." She turns enough to make space for the princesses next to her in the pile of bedding. Both young women quickly oblige, each mumbling praises to their 'Aunt Axa', as they snuggle up to her.

Nani still can't sleep. She looks up through the smoke flap to the stars beyond. The tepee is pitch black and her eyes haven't adjusted since the last embers of the fire imprinted their glow. The patch of night-sky framed by the opening sparkles like quartz. How beautiful is the Overworld.

Then she feels a chill wind, and a woeful dream wafts across her mind.

Why are there devils here tonight? Nani curses silently. Take your plagues, your fear, and your soldiers back to the Underworld. Soft skin is lifting into pockmarked warts all over our bodies. Tear down those new spiked fences from around the grain store. Get off those horses and pay respect to local customs. Pull off those badges of rank and burn them in the sacred fire. Wichita princes and Kuruk be hunters… please don't be fighters.

"Are you missing Ona?" Axa whispers. She doesn't want to wake Nana, if she has already found sleep. Indeed, Nana has been plucked from this waking world, and has been carried away on the wings of dreams. She is blessed with no self-doubt or worry, so sleep and dreams come as easily as waking and working.

Nani though, is a troubled mind, always being nosy.

Her soul is restless like a waterfall. Sometimes the flow of her thoughts become eddies, swirling around and bubbling in the centre, as ideas are swallowed up and swept away.

"I don't know," Nani whispers back to Axa, keeping her devils to herself. "I don't think of Mama all the time, as I know she's with me in spirit and I feel her all around and inside me. Still there is a space. She is here now...but I cannot touch her. I miss touching her."

"I, Aunt Axa, am here. Go to sleep now, as there are several days of duty ahead of us." She kisses Nani's forehead and they drift off to sleep.

LUCA

Marco is up before sunrise as usual, but this morning he is tingling with suspense. A special guest called Luca duly arrives, to accompany the Santee group to the Appalachi muster. Rumour has it that he knows about Marco, the Spanish newcomer.

The guest's skin is young but his gaze is old, and he wears a mixture of tribal and sailor clothing. He says he was taken by the sailor tribes earlier that year, but had since escaped back to his Chicora homeland.

When Marco sees him, he is uneasy at first. Does he know this man? Is this the Indian with Captain Cadiz in the courtroom? He looks quite different, with his long hair loose rather than tied - dressed more like a brave than a Spaniard.

Marco laughs nervously when he hears Luca introduce himself. Then he splutters in the Appalachi tongue. "Pardon me. That was very rude. Luca is also a Spanish name."

"Apology accepted, Senor De Serena," Luca parries in perfect Spanish, smiling at Marco.

"I never expected to hear that name again," Marco splutters in Spanish.

If, as it seems, 'Luca' from the courtroom and this Luca are one and the same, he will know of Marco's arrest on that earlier voyage. They have a lot to talk about but need to take care, because they are both guests of the Santee in one way or another, and they don't want to be seen plotting.

The twin princesses go to get consent to bring Marco and Luca to the Appalachi muster, and Axa urges the two young men to go fishing together in one of the streams that cross the gathering site.

"Luca is a very important name in Spanish," Marco watches Luca wading along the bank, feeling for catfish burrows.

"Thank you Senor," He pulls his arm out from an underwater burrow, without a river monster trying to swallow his hand. "The catfish aren't hungry today."

This brave hadn't changed much while away with the Spanish, despite some Spanish quirks. Marco is eager to know just what happened when Luca and a group of locals from the Calusa tribe were taken aboard Marco's ship. He had been in the cells and he only knows that they made it back to Dominica, where he was put on trial.

Marco tries to gain Luca's trust. "I understand the Calusa tribe is made up of clans who live on the coast."

"That's true, but they can barely be called a tribe. The swamps mean they don't mingle as we do."

"It's rumoured that your group were tempted aboard my ship by Captain Cadiz, with promises of a better life in other lands. Other stories say you were captured, or that you were lost at sea."

Luca doesn't reply and they sit together on the riverbank watching a heron waiting for its moment to strike at a passing fish. In the empty moment, Luca breaks the silence.

"Marco, you can ask about the past. Ask about Captain Cadiz." He is good at dodging difficult matters, and focussing on Cadiz will lead Marco away from the issue of the Calusa adventurers.

"Luca, I was in shame, but you were an honoured guest," he steers the exchange back to Luca's past.

"We were tricked, I suppose."

They dance around the issue of the Calusa passengers like boys, and their gaze falls again on the heron. In a flash, it strikes like an assassin and gulps the fish, then lazily lifts off across the reeds. The moment has gone and their trance is lifted on the broad wings of the huge bird. Those wings also waft away the urgency of probing each other for facts, and they wander back from their fishing empty-handed.

On their way back to the tepee, Luca remembers he is there for a purpose, and two issues meet on his tongue – one from his incredible but troubled life as an adventurer, and the other from his tribal upbringing. The first asks when and how they should murder Axa, the devil queen... and the second asks about Spanish bondage. The second matter of slavery comes out first. Perhaps the matter of murder can come later.

"Marco, what is the meaning of this trade in human souls?" Luca lowers his head in shame for talking about it.

Marco is taken aback, dropping the line and lures he is holding.

As if the gods interrupt, a drum calls them back to the Santee camp for news about their attendance at the Appalachi muster. The two men look at each other, shrug, and then laugh. Some spirit has cursed their trade in secrets for now. Luca's question about slavery and Marco's earlier questions about the Calusa braves can wait for another time.

For Luca, the matter of Axa's murder also waits in the shadows. A Spanish twitch pulls at his cheek like a fish being hooked, pulling him back. His double-life will get him into severe trouble one day.

"Are you careless or stupid?" his uncle used to say. He never understood that demand.

He knows he will be asked about the Spanish at this

gathering, but his knowledge of the Spanish should be traded, not given away. For now, he can hold onto the fact that Cadiz wants to start a war. Each bit of the plan can be traded in due course... how Cadiz will tell the Spanish empire about devil worship, and weaken the Indians with the plague. How he will get horses and outlaws to make the tribes blame each other for raids, and fight among themselves.

He need not reveal, just yet, that most of the Calusa braves who also went to Dominica had fallen sick within months; or that the Spanish governors paid him to say they were lost at sea, along with their Spanish comrades.

He laughed inwardly, as the Calusa leaders didn't believe their braves had sailed to the island of Dominica anyway. Many of the wizards thought the absent clan had been swept from their coast by a hurricane.

Luca knows mistrust. Only the old Governor, Juan Toledo, knew how long he had led a charmed life.

Six years earlier a younger, reckless Toledo found him as a young outcast who had canoed to his anchored ship. Toledo then sailed along the coast north of the great Creek River, and later told stories of the Creek monarchs being made giants at birth by the shaman. With Luca's help he chronicled the Indians as a race of men with tails like horses... and talked of the city of gold in the land of the Chicora people.

Toledo also introduced Luca to Captain De Leon, another wily explorer. With Luca's help, Leon intended to make a settlement in Florida, taking colonists, animals, and priests. To Luca's shame, there was no welcome from the Indians.

A striving Toledo then sent him to Madrid to be baptised, to describe the Indian culture to the court chroniclers, and to meet the King.

Those fantastic months in the Overworld of Spain had led to years of awkwardness as a double agent... to many trips back and forth across the storm-lashed seas around Florida... and now to his latest contract with Captain Cadiz.

Toledo's fatherly sway over him had soon led to a life of mercenary causes for Luca, just as the legends foretold the life of Cast-Outs. This time he had escaped the latest voyage during a shipwreck on a sandbank. Again, his own Chicora tribe and the Santee had accepted him back... but Cadiz had sworn him to murder the slave girl with the three sixes of the devil carved on her forehead.

He had vowed - in the name of his Christian god - to kill the Ashanti woman he was here to serve. Can Marco be trusted to help? Luca needs to be patient and see if this Spaniard also wants to serve Cadiz – getting rid of Axa, and starting a war.

EXPEDITIONS

On hearing Luca's story about escaping from the Spanish, Axa decides to let Kuruk know as soon as possible. Kuruk is both her suitor and an envoy of the Pensacola – a tribe who are proud of their long history with sailor voyages. She hails him with their agreed call and greets him in the nearby grotto.

"Prince Kuruk, I am sorry our meeting last night was awkward." Axa uses formal tongue and signs.

In the most secret part of her mind it had been easier to sit with him and not talk... just watch the princesses, to chuckle, and be together. He could take her mind off things at this gathering... in case Luca's story brings back bad memories.

Kuruk does a gallant nod.

"Aunt Axa, it was pleasing to meet you in the moonlight," he growls like the far-off rapids. "Now you are even more beautiful in the morning, with no makeup."

Full of himself, flirty, and funny all at once. He is irresistible, but their time for making love will come another day. First, she wants facts before the Appalachi muster later that morning.

"What do you mean 'Aunt'?" she pushes him sideways, as they sit down on a grassy ledge. He bows gently under Axa's friendly shove, and springs back upright. If she were his aunt, she wouldn't let him out until he had learned some manners.

They don't have much time, so she asks him about the Spanish. Kuruk is charming but also civil and she has weighty matters to discuss. His time with her will come eventually, so he painstakingly recounts what he knows.

"Princess Axa, you know that my Pensacola tribe

have had more contact with the Spanish than anybody. Several voyages have come and gone where the Alabama and Mississippi rivers meet the sea. One was the source of Marco's family helmet."

Axa smiles, but at the remark about the Spanish helmet, a fist of panic punches her in the chest.

Beware Ashanti princess, the gods of blame, mistrust, and fear will be released to ride on the wind and sweep away the old balance forever. Among the bloodthirsty new legends, nobody will look for traces of peace. Freedom from the tyranny of fear will be crushed with wizardry and scorn.

She gulps and lowers her eyes long enough to regain her poise. Wherever you come from - fearful images - go back there. Then she manages to splutter through the grip that this horror has on her tongue.

"Kuruk, how did... how did Marco's ... how did the family helmet... find its way to the Santee?" Axa buries the meddling from the Underworld in her stomach. Kuruk assumes she has a hair in her mouth, and he politely ignores her difficulty.

"Our legends say the helmet belonged to his father Diego de Serena, who led a voyage twenty years ago."

"You know your legends well. Is your queen grooming you for storytelling?" She slams the door on infernal thoughts and forces out gentle feelings again.

"Perhaps she is. It would be a great honour. Axa, if it means I can meet you more often, I will keep every legend and never get a single detail wrong."

"Continue." She wants him to stop talking soon and start kissing. The rumbling of his voice - slowly and carefully re-telling the legends - is seducing her and removing her sense of duty layer by layer. He simmers with energy, shuffling his hips and waving his long arms eagerly while telling the story.

"At the mouth of the Alabama River, Captain De Serena sent a group ashore. It included the Celtic man who would one day become Inca's father, together with a Spanish sailor wearing the captain's helmet to make a good impact. Through Diego's eyeglass their greeting looked hostile and he left them."

Axa completely loses track of the story as Kuruk doodles in the sand in front of her with a stick. His tone drops when speaking of their abandonment. Axa wants to reassure him or make love to him, and both the sentiment and the desire come out together. She grabs the back of his neck with both hands, forcing a smothering kiss on his full, soft lips. Closing her eyes, she vows that they must find some real privacy, sooner rather than later.

"Kuruk, join me later on top of the pyramid behind my tepee. I will call you."

She hears drums calling the Appalachi queens and breaks away to get ready for the Appalachi muster, leaving him stunned and speechless.

At her tepee, Luca is loitering. From a distance, his shape is different - perhaps a little tense - and up closer she notices his brooding, unreadable look is somehow empty. What is it about this young man that sometimes seems so tired of the world, yet so eager at other times? He normally takes little interest in tribal customs, but he flicks his gaze to Axa's three-pronged stabbing weapon, strung to her lower back.

"Queen Axa, pardon my asking, but why do you wear the 'death star' to the gathering?"

Axa feels her nostrils flare, as if seeking out the scent

of an energy-rush in a predator about to pounce.

"Luca of the Chicora, I don't know what you mean."

There was no animal coiling to strike - only Luca. A reluctant squint gives away her wariness, with her eyelids flaring a moment later. Something is making her nervous. The languid Chicoran brave averts his gaze and continues.

"Your Ashanti weapon, the one at your back. We don't carry these and we don't need them. We are rarely surprised by numerous beasts, because our forests are not too dense."

"My friend, it is always there, so I don't even notice it. Our forests in Africa can be very dense, but it is more symbolic. We call it a mantis."

"My Queen, it has no other purpose than to injure or kill at close quarters. I think the gathering will not look kindly upon it."

"Luca, thank you for your kind advice, but Marco carries a pistol and he's not expected to use it. I will carry this weapon until it causes concern. With you as one of my scouts I will never need it."

"As you wish, my Queen. I will call it 'mantis' rather than 'death star' for the rest of time."

Luca wanders off, but with an ungainly rather than relaxed amble. He looks awkward, like a chameleon whose prey has just walked out of reach of its flashing tongue.

TROPHIES

Back at the same chambers used by the lovers the evening before, Axa, Marco, Luca, and the twins settle down for the Appalachi muster. As Ona had said, the Appalachi tribes gather before some selected envoys go to the main meeting.

The chambers have been carefully altered into a place of ritual. The drums that call everybody are now thrumming background music, and incense is burning a mixture of seedpods and spices. There are comings and goings, but by mid-morning a tribal group has settled in each of the chambers, with prayer-sticks, wall hangings, and bunting on show.

The hosts are careful to tidy, but not sweep or wipe the floors and walls - so spiders and sweat are undisturbed. Everything conspires to welcome the guests with layers of custom. Then, without warning, another trophy is grandly unveiled, as Kuruk's Pensacola tribe shows off their own Spanish helmet taken from a different voyage.

Could these metal Spanish helmets be foretelling Axa about male revolt? The Ashanti had mastered the art of casting bronze long ago, and some men were useful for this dirty work. Some even cackled about their new-found wizardry, but never in earshot of a woman.

It was often repeated by the older wizards, to the young men... 'For you to plot against the mothers is to invite a curse on you, your family, and your people.' Dire warnings would follow... 'You will never marry and you will be forced to seek new clans. News of your exile will travel faster than you by drum, so you traitors will never find a foster-tribe.'

Then the Pensacola queen makes a speech about

their helmet, showing off her knowledge of the Spanish.

"Seven summers ago the leadership in Dominica sent a voyage under Alonso de Pineda. Our canoeists bartered for this splendid metal hat."

Axa's stomach twists at the sight of the gleaming object. This is too much for a mortal soul with a twisted heart and a broken mind.

Jealous of the Pensacola trophy, the Chicora and Calusa envoys have an argument about the Spanish. Some male members of their entourage have slipped into their chambers and start an embarrassing squabble. These two tribes have had a simmering bigotry since the last gathering, where some royal match-making had not worked. Ever since, they had found any reason to argue, and claims about contact with newcomers were the latest cause.

"We saw them first," brag the northern clans.

"We made first contact," claim the southern clans.

To lift the embarrassment the muster stops for the afternoon and several smaller meetings begin. Axa breaks off, pretending to need a stretch, but her mind swirls with the wrecking effect of male pride. Curse the devil fear, she mutters to herself when out of sight, pacing between two willow trees by a stream. Then without warning she hurls both the knives from her waist-belt, one into each tree. In a low squat, she checks the knife on her lower leg, and the mantis at her back, before calmly recovering the other knives and making her way back to camp.

Marco, meanwhile, is reminded of life in rural Spain where meals, siestas, and informal meetings are done during this hottest part of the day. The different groups return to their tepees with a few envoys thinking of tribal matters, some considering trade, but most just enjoying the company. The calling, drumming, and general busyness of the morning subsides gradually.

"My Spanish friend," Luca says as he, Marco and the twins set off back to camp, "this is the time for cold-blooded spirits to take the stage, when insects and reptiles play a game of life and death and we warm-blooded creatures call a truce."

*

Axa stirs first from her siesta and has a moment to take in her new surroundings. The other tribes are arranged in small clearings spread out across a vast area of forest - further than even a soaring bird can see. Only the smoke from the hundreds of tepees gives away the sheer scale of the great annual gathering. From any vantage point, the forest seems to be a giant, simmering volcano and everywhere the sound of festivals rises with the smoke towers.

Ona had told Axa about a rocky outcrop with a spectacular view, and suggested she take Marco there at sunset.

Marco murmurs his praise when he sees the vista. "This place is alive with festivities for mile after mile. The ancient chambers and artefacts breathe centuries of custom from before history."

"What is history?" Axa asks.

"Well... I suppose it's the writing of legends."

"Writing legends is so open to lies. Our story-tellers take great pride in keeping the stories just as they have always been, staunch in every detail."

As the sun dips below the far-off horizon, Marco replies. "I'm not sure that our writing is as useful or trustworthy as your storytelling. Most Spanish people cannot read and there are so many tongues, so sign-language and pictures are more real."

He sings to himself, watching the ghostly plumes of smoke rising slowly, joining hands, and dancing towards the Overworld. Unfortunately, for Axa the sun's retreat invites the ghosts that bother her so deeply. The dancing smoke looks like children, at once beautiful and happy - but then mutating into scowling bullies. Marco moves off, and by the time he knows Axa isn't with him, she has gone into a fearful trance.

Smoke-angels, beware the shape-shifters. See the limbs of these smouldering images - before your very eyes, they become more twisted creatures. She squints and tries to think of angels. Please dance to the sounds of waterfalls and humming birds. Looking at the curtains of smoke hanging against the fading orange and purple sky, her hopes are dashed. Where do you come from, half-boy half-mantis, half-girl half-leech? Why do you become predators, ambushing your victims and sucking their blood?

Then the demon of Fear wriggles like a worm in Axa's ears, saying over and again... 'You need to protect your grain store. The others have their eyes on it' - 'You need to protect your grain store. The others have their eyes on it'.

"No," Axa pushes at the bad angel, "the protectors will attack the others and this will start a war."

"You cannot stop me." The spectre of Fear laughs in her face. "The wizards will cleanse the legends themselves and the long cycles of peace since the Dreamtime will be scratched from all storytelling. Songs and dances will be raped. Drawings and carvings will be destroyed, or they will be changed to worship Fear."

She keeps her torment to herself and clenches her hands, digging her nails into her palms as hard as she can.

"Axa, my lady, are you alright?" Marco asks as he turns to find her rubbing her arms strangely. By now, she holds her knives upward in each hand and is dragging the hilts along the veins in her out-turned forearms.

"I'm fine, thank you," she snaps back into the real world from an imaginary place where she was considering turning the knives around. Luckily, he interrupts her, so it doesn't matter what is happening in the entrails of her mind. He accepts her word that all is in order and sets off again... but her soul is in grave pain. She runs to catch up with him. Where she used to enjoy time to herself, now she is afraid of it. Instead, she should want the company of fame and relish the constant kindness and duty that goes with it. This might protect her from the darkness of solitude.

PYRAMID

Axa and Marco go back to the Santee clearing and wait for drums to call them again. There is no sign of Kuruk, and she remembers her agreement to meet him on top of the nearby burial mound that stands forty-feet high over their tepee, like a great caretaker of the ancient balance. Calling him, she hears his response from high above her.

She goes up the slope like a child hunting for a pot of honey. Scrambling hand over hand, her thoughts race her upwards - Kuruk pulls her one way towards being carefree lovers - everything else pulls her towards her duty to the Santee, her adopted tribe.

Reaching the grassy top, she finds herself above the canopy of the forest, where wizards have kept away the scrub.

"Here are your wings." Kuruk hands her an eagle feather out of nowhere. In all her excitement and breathless climbing, he has silently come around behind her.

"I cannot fly away with you right now. I have to be at the Appalachi muster again very soon." She takes the feather and looks across the top of the forest roof that is steaming gently as the sun gives way to the moon. "Oh Kuruk every night should be spent in a place like this. We can watch our world slowly turning away from the Sun God and read the stars instead."

He moves up close behind her and places his long hands around her narrow waist, so his fingers almost meet to form a ring.

"Pardon me princess," his warm breathing wafts around her ears. "Did you come here to talk about warnings in the night sky?"

She closes her eyes, her lips moving around words of

duty, but her mind is moving around Kuruk's body.

"Prince Kuruk, stories are being told of kings replacing queens, with raiding instead of sharing." She twists around within his giant hands and snuggles her face into his chest. Lifting her eyes to him, her tongue is still tying knots. "I know that giving in to fear has terrible costs."

She doesn't care that she isn't making any sense, flitting from one thing to another. His proud features are carved like a totem pole, as he looks down at the fading sunset in her eyes and the rising moonlight on her cheeks. Almost out of a sense of duty, he breaks his near silence.

"Meeting here, just you and me, it feels like nothing will ever change."

The far-off drums of his voice make Axa's legs feel weak, but he grips her more firmly round her waist. Then a real drum sounds the beat for the Appalachi muster to resume soon.

"Kuruk my love, I must go now but I want you right here when I get back. Guard my tepee, and when you hear me returning, come back to this exact spot and wait for me."

Marco and Luca notice Axa and Kuruk going up the pyramid, and Luca becomes nosy about the role of the burial mounds in Spain. He asks Marco about them as they stroll around the wide base of this edifice.

"You have mounds all over your countryside in Spain, but no legends or stories about them?"

"I spent most of my boyhood meeting girls by our stone circles, and we had battles with other gangs among the ancient village walls. Those sites are very old, but our legends only go back a few thousand years."

"We, the first peoples of this land, have been here

for a hundred thousand years." He claps the signs for these uncountable numbers. "I can show you paintings in our caves of animals that no longer walk the earth, but are entombed in the cliffs."

"Luca my friend," Marco is a bit tired of his lecturing, "I will ask the elders next time I am on my farm in Castile. The priests don't allow any talk about the ancient past, but we sometimes whisper about it over a glass of wine. First, show me around these Pensacola resting places of ancient queens."

"You will not find any gold."

"Very funny."

"My dear Marco, the mounds are still linked with the seasons. The same solstices you worship in Spain in your festivals. Many sites have buried trophies and artefacts, such as Spanish chain-mail from across the sea, and iron axe-heads traded from the north... but now I think we have a meeting with the other tribes."

Luca moves on, but Marco feels a chill as if the sun has gone down forever. The cold slaps him in the face and wraps him up so tight he can hardly breathe. The freezing air threatens to harden his lungs so he will die.

Spain and solstices, trophies and burials, words and symbols... these aren't signs of worlds apart... they are signs of worlds colliding. This 'new world' is older than anything left standing in the 'old world'. These people with their endless cycles have never changed - not since the Old Testament started counting the ancestors. Their place isn't alongside the newcomers. It's a different place altogether, in a different time, and there is no room for newcomers here.

Marco shakes his head and shivers to the core. Then he sees Luca marching on, so he breaks into a run to catch up, back towards the tepee.

Axa and Kuruk return from their short break together, while Luca and Marco are putting the tea things away. She is in a rare, almost blissful good humour, and the roosting of huge flocks of birds reflects the sense of togetherness.

Her happy mood goes hard when she sees that Marco is hollow. Has Luca upset him? She and Marco are from across the sea, while Luca claims to have been to Spain and back, switching spirit guides along the way. None of them belongs here like the others, but Marco seems happy to be among the First Peoples. He will always be a newcomer, but now an honoured one. Who knows what he is running from in his former life? Maybe Luca keeps Marco's darkest secrets – even darker than shipping captives across the sea. If nothing else, Marco is a deeply caring man with a troubled soul.

Luca for his part is holding back. He freely talks of his travels but it's never the full story. Unlike Marco, Luca is carefree... maybe because he cannot care. Maybe his soul is so buffeted that it has a defensive shell around it – made of scar tissue. On the other hand, maybe there is nothing inside the shell, nothing to guide him, and he has simply been caught up in amazing events.

Whatever it is, they are only men. They will have a part to play – but Mother Fate controls their future.

MURDER

For Luca, talking about the far off past with Marco was interesting but what about Captain Cadiz and the devil worship in the present? Finding a den near the grotto, he takes some special tea and dreams invade his mind, but they do not obey him, or help him focus on his task.

Thoughts eddy around of his childhood among the Chicora – running away as a young man - becoming famous among the Spanish - and now he is an envoy at this gathering.

The dreams of his recent shipwreck are the most powerful, and he can almost smell again the energy of the tempest. The horizon had rested under curtains of pink rain and yellow clearings, while a strip of spear-point grey cloud had crept closer. Above that, the towering anvil-clouds had girded their loins.

The sailors' only friend in the world – Father Sun – had retreated in the west. One by one the stars emerged, only to be smothered from the east in dense gloom, and still there was no wind.

Silent bursts of light, high in the darkness, had revealed the towers overhead. Their noiseless mountain-building piled heavy clouds on heavier seas, and by early morning the low rumbling of the anvils above became angry rants. Then the crash of great doors became the cannon fire he remembered from his trip to Spain, as the gods spat their fire ever closer to their flotilla.

All sails and hatches had been tied down with double knots and treble hitches. Wind and waves had joined the din of light and sound, tossing the souls of the crew who stayed in exile below deck. Bracing themselves, holding on, praying... their last hope had been the Master Shipwright and the timbers he had chosen for their womb

– hopefully not their sunken tomb.

After endless hours of hell, the sun had still hidden beyond the abyss. Glimpses through the timbers of what could be evening or morning had invited some hope, and the beating had stopped - but this had also happened in the eye of the storm. By the shards of light, it was morning and their view was east.

A whole day and night had been swept away and they dare not look west towards the storm, for fear of inviting it to return. They were high and dry on a sandbank and slowly they broke the shell of the vessel they had used to endure the Underworld. The palest hues of pink, orange and silver had rippled below a morning sky of lemon, mint, and purple. It had felt like they were dead, and in the afterlife.

Luca sobs, remembering the ruthless tide coming in, breaking up the ship, and his shipmates being dragged under by unseen water-monsters. They barely had time to scream, but their wide eyes and open mouths had cried out for their souls.

As he had clung to the flotsam and jetsam, even a drowning priest had shouted that god had left them to their fate. "This storm is the devil's work," were his last words. Luca had imagined that the tribal witches, with the help of the Ashanti princess, were cooking up a curse on the wind and wave.

That is why he is having this dream.

He hadn't pleaded to the gods for mercy, but he never had. Even when cast out from his tribe there was no feeling. Governor Toledo had become like a father to him after taking him aboard as a boy, but had lost interest when he found his young Indian brave so impregnable. When he sent Luca to Spain, had Toledo given up his quest to prove Florida was an island, or was he just trying to get rid of his native spy?

For Luca, even being baptised before the Holy Roman Emperor in the Overworld of Spain had left him unmoved, and in the company of Cadiz he never judged the wily captain, or reflected on right or wrong. Now Luca feels nothing as the dreams fly away, and he at last plans Axa's murder.

The Black Queen will not allow herself to be surprised in hand-to-hand combat. Her speed and her death-star - or 'mantis' weapon - make close-up murder extremely dangerous, if not impossible. It will take something else... what about poison? Perhaps a booby-trap, but that would leave evidence. A hunting accident could do it... a loose bow shot... how might that work?

No. It will have to be an ambush while she meditates. He might have a split second for a lethal arrow, before she smells or hears him, and he could use a Calusa shaft to cause the most turmoil.

Axa, if you are indeed Satan, then some godly spirit will surely see that the arrow flies true – and pierces your heart.

Perhaps this explains why fate sent Luca's wandering soul to the Overworld for baptism, and he will be saved from sin by returning to save his own people from this devil masked as an Ashanti Princess.

This must be his calling.

His mother's dreamy voice interrupts this fantasy. 'Luca dear, go and play with your sisters.' He always did what he was told, but he never understood the reasons... so why was he banished for what happened to his younger sister – after all, accidents happen?

SUMMONS

Axa is fetching a coat to guard against the evening chill, when some unexpected visitors arrive. Jay and Chet are being led into the clearing by scouts who can hardly conceal their shock.

Her mind grasps for some urgent reason. Jay is much less hot-headed since her shame as a traitor those many moons ago. She was completely pardoned and is one of the Santee's best ambassadors, but what is she doing here? She and Chet have been trusted with helping Ona perform the rituals of the tribe back home. Marco and Luca greet them first, while Axa chews her tongue. With the older twin princesses both here at the gathering, Jay and Chet should never have left the tribe for any reason. There are many other good scouts to bear messages back and forth, and if it is urgent there are the drums.

Straight away, the older twins start teasing Jay.

"Who is this in the guise of my sister?" Nani starts.

"It is Anansi the spider. You don't fool us," Nana joins in.

It is a routine they have used to bait Jay all her life, but given a new twist by the spider stories that Axa has brought from Africa. The twins will prattle on, more like two witches than heirs to queenly status, so Axa stops any more ranting by raising her hand. She hopes Jay will not rise to the bait, but she is completely unruffled by the goading and comes straight to the point.

"Axa, there are two other Spanish ships, and this time they are making camp."

Everybody draws breath. Jay's news of the sailors making a colony could change everything, and it will certainly affect which tribe will speak at the Grand Council later. None of the coastal peoples are talking of settlements or colonies being built by the newcomers, or at least not openly. That has never happened before.

Leaving Jay and Chet, Axa leads the Santee group of the twins, Axa, Marco and Luca back to the Appalachi muster. The full moon has replaced the sun with its cooler reflected light, but to Santee eyes it is as good as daylight. She pauses, recalling the full moon when she first came ashore in this land. Briefly the nightmare of the voyage comes back. The combined stories of Marco, Luca, and now Jay could mean that her sisters and cousins have returned on Spanish ships, and will still be in captivity at the new colony.

Marco manages to speak to Axa alone just before the Santee group get to the muster chambers.

"Axa, I don't know how to ask you, but the gathering will want to know my place among the Santee."

He never dared ask about his status in the tribal community and was content to build a new life. It was a life he thought was over before the wolf attack, and his time since then seemed to be part of a dream. Had his father's helmet saved him from death, and was this God's choice? Now the basic matter of 'What kind of man am I?' needed to be asked. Does he have a role in the tribe, or is he just another newcomer?

Axa is curt.

"The gathering isn't a single being, but it is made up of many queens with many traits. Most of them aren't interested in Santee affairs, or the status of a newcomer."

You are a 'newcomer' too, he thinks. Then he scolds himself for forgetting that she is now a queen on both sides of the Atlantic.

"Axa, I am cursed with my former life but I cannot change it. If I had brought only skills and trade, I could hold my head high... as earlier voyages have done. I cannot escape my guilt in front of you, but I cannot remain its prisoner forever. To everyone else I am pardoned as a mere thief, but to you I remain unpardoned... as a Spanish slaver."

"Do not say that word." Axa barks, finally looking directly at him. "There's no such thing as a... I will not say it." She turns her back on him. "A soul is always free."

He straightens his back and looks into the distance as if standing on a parade square. "I will be the prisoner of my shame for as long as you have a use for me."

Then he falls to his knees in tears. She already knows what use she has for him, if not his exact role. Luck has brought her and Marco to the Santee, to sway the gathering to do something about the Spanish – but she should not interfere too much with the flow of signs and chances that are unravelling for her.

"Let the river run its course," her mother used to say.

She turns around to face him again - still on his knees - and lowers her tone in sympathy. Understanding his pain at carrying such a curse, in this life and maybe the next, she tips her head downward and addresses him directly.

"Once this matter of the Spanish in the east has been resolved then you can go, and I hope you find peace. I will not reveal your past - that is for the spirits of justice. For now I need to be focused on more important matters."

SAILORS

The Appalachi muster finally resumes and the main concern is that the sailor tribes have no women. Some tribal wizards are badgering their Clan Mothers about the lack of Kristiano queens, and the Pawnee have sent men to this gathering in response to the stories about the newcomers. Some tribes have even sent wizards as chiefs, doubting the queenly system of order.

Axa's mind goes back to Africa...

"Dear Axa," her mother would say, "While the men hunt, women do the useful things - like trapping, gathering, and growing. It is the women who know how to make shelters, textiles, and pots."

The Clan Mothers of the Ashanti often sang to the young girls about women keeping the legends, knowing the seasons, and regenerating their tribe. Axa's youthful mind found the reasons for female royalty were compelling... "Princess, women carry the status and the female line is always known."

Painfully, she must return to the here and now.

Sitting in the front of their sunken chambers, the seated envoys are more solemn and withdrawn than they were earlier. Lit by the central fire, Axa and the other three queens are glowing against their outsized shadows - cast on the walls behind them.

"What is the truth about the newcomers?" asks the Calusa queen, before a pregnant pause wraps the group. Her stress on the word 'truth' suggests that she has heard many rumours about the Spanish, but hasn't made up her mind about them. She fiddles with one of her earrings as she waits for someone to answer. Axa rises, and she talks to the group with sign language and Santee tongue,

"Our wizards fear stories of evil among the sailors,

but they ignore the trade and skills they have brought with them." Her mouth fills with spit with the effort of being fair to the Spanish, but she swallows it down.

"In the sailor tribes," Luca adds, when asked by a gesture from Axa, "the men are powerful."

He has simply stated something that is already clear. Axa flicks her eyebrows at him, but he doesn't flinch. Repeating the slight wave that she used to get him started, he still looks blank.

"Luca."

"They take whatever and whoever they want." The words rush out like a dam has broken. "I am proof of this slavery, and the treachery of the sailors."

His fantasies about killing Axa in the name of God are a far-off memory. He has changed sides again… always running with the pack, whether the hunter or the hunted. In this place, he runs with the hunted… for now anyway.

Marco takes over in motley signs and limited Santee phrasing. "Queens cannot pow-wow with these princes. If we offer our princesses, they will see this as weakness."

Axa then sums things up, now going with the flow of disapproval.

"So, mustered queens, there's a male revolt among our northern peoples, and the threat of captivity."

"Queen Axa of the Santee," the Chicora queen announces, "you will be sent to the Grand Council to explain this."

It is now very late and after some other less important matters, the Appalachi muster breaks up. A rumbling of unhappiness grips the envoys as they leave.

Axa hears a call from Jay and replies for her to come and join them as they go back to their camp.

"Jay, I thought you might be here, keen to know

what the meeting had to say."

"Are you angry with me?"

"What use would that be? You are your own woman. Let's drop back and talk in private."

Marco, Luca, and the twins go on ahead.

Axa takes hold of Jay's hand as they walk, and grips it as if she is holding onto her last hope of peace.

"With us here," Axa says, "why did you leave Ona?"

"The All-Seeing Eye told me to go south, and that is where I found out about the Kristianos building a camp."

Jay shakes off Axa's grip.

"Axa, are you alright?"

Axa's eyes have begun to stream with tears, but she holds back any sobbing behind tightly pursed lips. Then, with a long, deep breath she manages to say, "I was like you. I had plans to marry and make my mother a grandmother." Head bowed she continues walking and talking but with her tears falling off her face. "You should spend as much time with your mother as you can."

"Ona is not in danger and her illness has been leeched away."

"She is not in danger now, but these are changing times. You can never get back the lost time with her."

Jay jumps in front and as Axa stumbles, wraps her arms in a bear hug.

"Dear Axa, pull yourself together."

Axa laughs as her arms are pinned to her sides in the moonlight., and Jay kisses the salty tears off her down-turned face

"Our Ashanti Princess cannot be seen crying at a gathering!" Jay says, before pulling Axa along to catch up with the others.

When Axa and the twins get back to their tepee, Kuruk hears them coming and slips away as planned.

Axa's thoughts turn to him waiting on top of their giant love nest. She again scrambles up the pyramid and he again welcomes her with a rampant embrace.

"Kuruk, your name means tempest, but you make me feel safe, and I feel happier than I have ever felt in this land. You are no tempest, but a cool summer breeze blowing over me."

"What is it Axa? Is something wrong?"

"My love, I think you overheard Jay and Chet bring news of a Spanish colony. It may include my people. It may include my fiancé."

There is a long, empty silence and Axa feels the chill of the night as they sit down cross-legged in front of each other. Her hands find their way into a praying pose, where Kuruk squashes them gently in the palms of his own prayer.

"Axa my love, these last few days of fleeting moments with you have opened my eyes. I love you, and my fire burns for you whatever you decide to do." He wraps her up in his arms and legs and wraps them both in the big fur blanket he has brought with him.

"Oh Kuruk," Axa murmurs, as she wishes he would throw her over his shoulders and carry her away, "give me another day to deserve your love. Please be back here again tomorrow night, when I will have had time to understand all of this."

They silently watch the Milky Way sweeping by, and then go back to their own tepee for some lonely, aching sleep.

AFTERLIFE

The next day Axa, Marco, and Luca are called to act for the south-eastern peoples at the Grand Council a short ride away, leaving the twin princesses behind with the other Appalachi groups. It is unusual to take three envoys, but Axa will need her chief witnesses... Marco was a sailor, and Luca claimed to have gone with the sailors to their island base. They will have to explain the prospects or the threat of the sailors to satisfy the whole gathering.

Luca nudges his horse forwards. "Axa, I am not sure I am worthy of a call up from the Grand Council."

Marco's horse always walks behind, much to his annoyance. It gives Axa and Luca a chance to talk privately, as their horses walk happily two abreast.

"Luca, stop grovelling. You know what I went through, and I thank you for keeping it a secret. Between us, we must state truthfully about the Spanish. I'm not sure I can do that alone, and you have a fuller story."

Luca straightens on the horse, proud of himself but also because his animal is nervous. He has been flattered as an adventurer by the Spanish, but never enjoyed true respect among his people.

"My queen, the legends tell how our tribes were made of smaller clans, and how they came together. Then how we became part of the Appalachi group by joining with the Calusa and Alabama peoples. I cannot see this with the Spanish."

"Is there no common ground, no shared profit in the long run?" Axa asks, more in hope than belief.

Luca has longed to prove his worth, and he has rehearsed his judgement on both cultures. His horse snorts as he continues... "There are good men and women in Spain, but their leaders and priests conjure up a fear of the afterlife."

"What is their afterlife?" Axa rubs her forehead and drags her hand down her face.

Luca is under her spell. "It isn't another life as we think. It is paradise, but you can only go there by joining their tribe. They say the soul and the body have different fates, while we imagine they are one. They see what makes things different - people and animals, good and bad, life and death, while we trust that everything is woven together, in balance."

"You are very clever, I will tell your queen. Now why would we need the paradise of which you spoke?"

"We don't. We live in paradise already, where being reborn makes us improve ourselves." He sums up the problem without attempting to explain it. They are two totally unmatchable beliefs. "At the gates of their paradise they are pardoned for their sins. There is forgiveness for almost any atrocity in the name of spreading their beliefs."

"Forgiveness?"

Luca imagines his standing once Axa tells his monarch how useful he is. "Axa, we can only make up for our wrongs by putting them right. Otherwise, we take our crimes into the next life. That could be as a mangy coyote." He pictures Marco's future, if he doesn't put right his misdeeds.

"How do they get forgiveness?"

"By confessing to their priests just before the afterlife. There's no need to put things right in this life." He shakes his head.

Axa frowns. Then the full impact of the Spanish beliefs hit home. "So a person can do terrible wrong if it is in the name of their god. Equally, they can be forgiven forever, simply by confessing. They have little reason to do any good - to tolerate or to share in this life. There's nothing to stop them using us for the sake of worthless trophies."

Luca had once hoped to tell his own Chicoran queen his ideas, but was never invited to do so. Now this foreign queen gives him his chance. "Their people are good. They think we are all equal before the creator, and in loving their neighbours - but their leaders think that personal glory will glorify their god. This pursuit of riches, glory, and blessings in the afterlife will make them push us ever higher into the mountains."

"Eagle help me to see. I must gain the respect and trust of the gathering, while at the same time giving them this stark warning."

Axa's stomach feels empty and all she can do is pray to the gods of this new land... All-Seeing Eye, what lies in the west? Whatever awaits us, protect the Santee and other tribes under your powerful gaze. Show this Ashanti princess what to do in this body, and her next life will be as a higher being.

PERSUASION

At the Grand Councils of the past, the other queens have admired and loved Ona, and her many adventures and feats are part of the stories of the Great Basin groups in general. The story of her only ever 'miss' in an archery contest is painted on her tepee... when all her other shots were in the bullseye, she shot a lizard on the edge of the target.

Ona's twin daughters are respected though not ready for leadership. So only Axa, Marco, and Luca have been summoned - but not for their status. They are too new, too strange, and too mixed up with the sailor tribes. However, by Ona's decree, Axa is the voice of the Santee until the twins are older, while Marco and Luca are key witnesses.

Riding to the Grand Council chambers, Luca has just revealed all he seems to know about the Spanish, but Axa smells conflict within him and notes his slight stutter.

"Axa, the council will... they will want to know about a trade in goods, if not ideas. No doubt some of the wizards are interested in the pistols and muskets." His horse is still behaving as if some large predator is nearby.

"These horses should mind their own business," she protests, patting hers on the neck and returning to Luca's point, "My own Ashanti people have traded gold for weapons, with terrible results."

She notices him stiffen again. Horse and rider are both riding on thin ice.

"My Queen, we have little tin or gold but the Spanish don't know that, and they will offer their skills and new crops for us to try. Nevertheless, it is the threat of the colony, or Catholic Mission, that worries me most." Luca's horse tosses its head angrily. His tongue has been loosened by Axa's charm while his limbs are heavy – like a guilty child.

"Yes Luca, we have seen in Africa that they have another plan… to convert us to their god. This will give them an excuse to gain a foothold and then use us. We must persuade the ancient council of the danger."

Luca's mount is now so jittery that he is becoming embarrassed, and Axa raises her hand to show it is time to find somewhere to leave the horses. Luca gladly takes his beast back up the path to meet Marco, in the hope it will settle down.

Axa has a few minutes to herself – long enough for the Spanish threat to dawn on her like a blood-red sunrise. Will this ancient culture see the warning signs? Ona said that the Grand Council has been part of the cycles since the Dreamtime – with deeply shared values, felt through fired-clay artefacts that had been traded forever.

"Bless the power of peace," Ona had said while they visited a shrine, "half-human figures in seated poses have travelled across the land to tell the story of thousands of gatherings."

Axa shakes her head. These are signs of timeless support. They hammer copper and carve rock, always showing people working together. This will blind them to new threats unless there are clear signs of danger.

Luca and Marco walk up to her but she waves them on, pretending to be settling her horse.

"Go on, I will catch up."

She doesn't make eye contact and they don't notice she is in a cold sweat. Frantic for signs, she looks for warnings in Ona's stories of the cosmos, which had been so similar to Ashanti beliefs.

"Axa my dear, the Overworld is the home of the

Sun, Moon, and Morning Star representing order and stability. The Middleworld is where we live, and the Underworld is a cold, dark place of chaos... home to the old woman who never dies." Ona had pointed to a large painting in a cave, "These worlds are connected by an axis, such as a cedar tree or a striped pole."

How can she persuade the council that the Spanish are from the Underworld and that the male-only newcomers who conceal chaos should not be invited into the Middleworld?

Ona's words come flooding back. "The Underwolds and Overworlds fight constantly, but queenly rituals soothe these powerful forces. Each clan uses sacred figurines, kept in shrines on top of the mounds where they can watch over us."

Now the mounds symbolise her feelings for Kuruk... that their love should rise above the people and the forest, and reach to the heavens.

They all finally reach the Grand Council circle and she pauses to give Luca some counsel. He is at last more comfortable in his own skin – away from his horse.

"Luca, our time has come to bear witness to the newcomer issue, but we must wait our turn. We may not be called upon for hours, or we may be first to speak. Either way, we must go with the flow and not give in to our own ideas."

"Like the Grand Council in Madrid," Luca smirks, "or those African councils that you told me about."

"The same. Like those councils, we must accept what they say. Our own time with the Spanish - even yours from so many travels - is only part of the picture. In this life, we must say what we have seen, and in the next life we will reap the rewards of honesty. We must not let fear rule our heads, or that devil will rule us instead."

Luca is speared by respect and guilt in the same moment. God, is this your choice? These new feelings – regard for Axa and shame at cursing her – must be spirits. He remembers his uncle saying people are all equal, 'A person is a person when they see others as persons'. Perhaps Luca did have feelings before his banishment as a boy. Maybe this woman, who he has carelessly sworn to kill, is a true heir to the ancient wisdoms. His vow in another god's name is being slain.

MERCENARY

Luca's mind goes back to the bar in Dominica, and the drunken hectoring of Captain Cadiz. He hears the echoes of the plan to start a war in simple stages...

Claim that the spirals idolise Satan;

release Pestilence, War, Famine, and Death on horseback;

and let raiding by Cast-outs destroy the ancient trust between the tribes.

Soon they will be weakened by the plague and fight among themselves. A small Spanish garrison could march on their capitals and defeat their depleted armies, just like the Aztec.

Then he remembers his own stupid, drunken boast. His words come back to him... "I swear, in the name of God, I will not rest until I have killed the devil in her."

Was he cursed by greedy causes? Will he be an outcast forever – or can he be accepted back, and be one with the spirals and the mother again?

Luca's mind is far away when Marco speaks.

"Axa, will I be called to give evidence?"

Axa doesn't reply. In truth, she doesn't know. He is a trophy and could give vital facts, but he is also a runaway from the Spanish. It could go either way.

The council circle is draped in banners depicting the customs of their tribes. For Marco it is a bewitching sight but for Luca and Axa, it is full of spirit power. He notes the upbeat energy.

"Queen Axa, the symbols are renewing their bonds."

"I hope all these signs remind the meeting of its purpose - to maintain the balance."

"That's true, but the meeting is quick to get to business. I was a runner at a gathering as a boy. The whole festival always begins and ends with ceremonies, while the council meetings aren't hampered by courtesy."

To their surprise, Axa and the Santee group are at once called from their half-buried chamber, out to the sun-drenched patio. The Mistress of the Ceremony wears a tattooed face and body, with solid and dotted lines and circles. Her clothes are modest, made of tanned hides, but they are highly decorated in elk-teeth and shells. She loudly announces the matter at hand is the sailor tribe and steps aside.

Luca shyly observes each of the other queens in minute detail. They are all practiced to reveal little of their thoughts or feelings, and he relies on mere flickers to see behind the masks.

Each queen and all their consorts have already admired Axa's scars – made at birth. The three spirals on her temple glisten, and sing of trust in the Mother. In the northern chamber, the queen's gaze is direct and unblinking, but there is concern in the way she tucks her chin and closes her nostrils.

The queen in the western room is more relaxed, and nearer to Axa in age. She tips her head slightly and the tiniest dimples hint at a smile.

In the southern space the queen is much older, and she has a face so wrinkled that even Luca cannot fathom her feelings from among its folds.

One thing is clear from their manner - they want to get on with things quickly and get back to local festivals as soon as possible. None of them doubts that Ona's wisdom is with Axa, and that the other Appalachi tribes have agreed to this.

From each surrounding chamber in turn come the questions. The first, from the troublesome northern Kiowa is typically direct, and a wizard sits behind their queen.

"Do they take our braves?"

Silence. This does at least point to the most important matter at hand.

Luca steps forward.

"Yes. My Calusa friends and I show that."

"Luca, we are told that you asked to go, and you were well-treated," is the challenge from the usually friendly Navajo, representing the western area.

Yes - Luca thinks without reply - but most of those Calusa braves died of disease. The secret of their deaths is still concealed in the lie about being drowned.

Marco breaks the new silence.

"No. They don't steal people from your tribes, but they do bring Africans."

"Why would anybody want that?" is the next question, this time from the Apache representing the Great Plains.

Another silence stretches longer than is polite and is only interrupted by a bumblebee drifting into the chamber. They are losing momentum, and the point of the Spanish threat is fizzling out when Axa grabs Marco by the shoulder.

"I myself have been a captive, kidnapped by this Spanish adventurer."

DECISION

The Grand Council is surprised, but not as shocked as Marco. "I will not reveal your past," Axa had sworn a few hours earlier. Now he will always be a slave to his past, as much as Axa had briefly been a slave to the Spanish empire. He swallows hard and lifts his eyes skyward. How long before his exposed throat feels a blade from ear to ear?

After a few moments of silence, the patio and chambers become a bustling market of messages being passed back and forth by the runners.

Luca manages to absorb the surprise announcement and see the next steps at the same time.

"Queen Axa, soon the Mistress of Ceremonies will be able to deliver the agreement about the Spanish colony," he whispers in Axa's ear.

The Mistress speaks the main languages of the basin cultures, drawing and acting if necessary, and allowing time for accounts in the tongue of each of the chambers. The message is simple.

"The sailors aren't welcome. Axa is proof of a trade in human souls and Marco is proof of treachery, switching from the Spanish side to the side of our peoples at will. Their metals and crops aren't needed, and nor is their explosive pipe. The Santee can deter trade and limit any new footholds in the coastal lands, with the Calusa's help, if needed. This should be done in the spirit of honest pow-wow, or they can send for help using drums, if brutality is needed."

The mistress adds that such methods have always worked before, and the signs are good this time... "Many moons have come around since Axa got here and Luca was taken. This latest visit from the sailors has left one ship run-aground at the mouth of the Santee River, and only two ships landed somewhere to the south of there."

Luca then talks of the flotilla in detail - with some fine drawings on the dirt floor. "The Calusa kept back some facts about the colony-building, but since Jay's news they have told me more. They state that many Africans are among the landing party."

He has thrown all he knows behind Axa's cause, even if it snubs his friends among the Calusa. Like a sail flip-flopping in the eye of a storm, he goes whichever way the wind is blowing at that moment.

During a short break, Marco chooses to speak to Axa about the Africans. For better or worse, he raises the taboo subject that their months of sharing a new life among a new tribe haven't allowed them to confront. Each has spared the other – and each has chosen to avoid this issue ever since.

"Axa, after your announcement about kidnap, I am hostage to the curse of my former life, but I could lift this torment by helping you free your African people." He throws all his cards on the table.

Axa thinks for a moment how brave or how reckless he is to waylay her now, and how a weaker man would choose to run away again.

"This isn't the time or place for this, Spaniard."

"No my lady, I will wait on your choice. You can be assured of my faithfulness." He speaks with his head bowed.

Is he thinking about his next life in the Santee way, instead of the Spanish afterlife? Perhaps he could help free her African people and face the end of this life - whenever it came - with an open heart.

The meeting soon resumes about other matters, and hotly debates the matter of manners when horses are ridden. The more nomadic tribes are keen to breed more horses, because they would be very useful on the open plains. Then there is a new problem - some Cast-Out braves are using horses and forming larger groups – then they are forcefully trading arrowheads for rare foods.

The Santee group aren't listening and Axa picks at the cuticles behind her fingernails. She hunches away from where Marco sits over her shoulder, trying to ignore the echo of his remark: 'I could help you free your African people.' What chance led him back to her and meant he could now be so important? Perhaps that is why Ona had bound them as siblings, and spirits have led Luca and even Chet to trust him.

Marco's commitment to the Santee seemed sincere, but he is a man and has no true guide through the maze that Mother Fate has set for them. If he changes sides again, he could unleash the plagues of fear brought by the newcomers. Maybe she misread the signs - and she should have executed him before the wolf attack.

Among the other delegates, there are a few statements about sharing resources until the winters get back to normal; about pardons for Cast-Outs; and about trading horses - then Axa and the others make their way back to the Santee camp.

It is evening again, so Marco and Luca go mingling, while the twins go to find the Wichita princes.

Returning alone to the tepee, Axa finds Kuruk is making himself at home. Maybe he is dreaming of sharing her tepee on the Santee River, being in love, and raising a family. The same thought crosses her mind - seeing him so at home among her things - but she fidgets as she speaks.

"My dear Kuruk, have you heard the choice of the Grand Council?" He nods slowly. "I have decided that only the smallest group will try to dislodge the Spanish camp. We will leave as soon as possible, but first there's the other great feature of the gatherings... the corn dance."

She is about to say that this gives them the chance to slip away and have a few days together, just the two of them.

"Yes my queen," he nods again, "these customs are older than the councils themselves. We gather at the end of the maize harvest and place the green corn in the huge earth ovens, before cooking it over several days."

Why is he being so formal again? We stopped playing that game after that first kiss.

"What's the matter Kuruk? You don't need to be the keeper of the legends today."

He looks at her with his mouth downturned. "I also heard that you made a statement about Marco de Serena... about your past...."

"What past?" She has never been in this position before, as only Marco and Ona have known about her captivity. Now she has revealed her imprisonment to the Grand Council, this will change her status among her new family forever.

"Princess, don't be angry. I just want to know more about the woman I love."

"Love me, now. Not my past, or anybody or anything else." Axa is on fire with a sense of wrong. Damn curse of lies - why, on the brink of finding happiness - on the brink of desire - should anything matter but the future? She grabs him by the waist and pulls him down on top of her. They make love, and for one night only the world stops turning.

The opposite forces are working for the twin princesses that night. The world is turning ever faster as they find the Wichita princes with rendezvous calls and the four of them set off for the scout camp. They spend the night there dancing and smoking, much to the amazement of the ordinary revellers who do not expect royalty at a scout camp. At sunrise they return to their tepee where Axa is now alone.

"Aunt Axa," Nana asks gently, "where's Kuruk?"

"Nana, Nani, I will thank you for being quiet about Kuruk… about the two of us. We are in love, and I have asked him to go to Ona and seek her consent to make a home with me."

The twins are surprised that she needs Ona's consent, and they see a chance to kill two birds with one stone.

Nani speaks first. "Aunt Axa, your love for Kuruk is safe with us and you will be very happy together. Perhaps Kuruk can also raise the matter of our new Wichita princes. We want to make homes with them too."

Nana joins in. "We can have three motherly tepee in a cluster at the edge of the village, and be left to raise our families. Surely the gods will look kindly on such an idea."

"Come here my loves," Axa hugs them both. "You must now take part in the green corn festival on behalf of the Santee, while I get some rest before going to the Spanish colony. Then we can raise families, and we can have the biggest festival since the Dreamtime."

MISSION AMERICA

118

PART THREE

MISSION

ALLIANCE

The corn ceremony ends under the watchful eye of the sunrise, and Axa wakes up not sure of where she is. Sleeping and waking thoughts mingle, before she remembers that she was forced to come to this new land. Her kidnap is no longer a secret.

In the women's tepee, while the twins sleep, Ona returns to Axa in a dream.

"Ona, after what I said at the Grand Council, everybody knows that Marco kidnapped me but then released me from slavery. I am truly sorry that I never told you the whole truth."

"Beloved Axa," Ona's echo wipes a tear, "I cannot imagine your ordeal in that other world. I am not sure our myths can help with those demons. Instead I can help you control them, at least until we have new guidance."

The image of Axa's mother appears and warily raises the subject of the family curse – of terrible moods. "Dear Axa, your uncle thought he had a lizard in his head who kept his worst fears. Usually the reptile listened to the birds circling his mind, but if it was surprised it would shun them, and keep the fear to itself."

"Mother, did he learn to calm this lizard?"

"Sometimes, my dear. Then sometimes it would dart about in fright for no clear reason… perhaps a smell or a sound… "

Ona interrupts. "Axa, don't fight it. Live with it… even love it… until we can know it. Santee angels will find a way."

"Thank you both. I love you." Axa ends the exchange with the usual tenderness. She is now settled with the twists of fate that have brought her here, and for once her demons don't interfere with her inner peace.

While preparing to move out, Chet wonders if Marco harbours some loyalty to the Spanish colony, and despite their hangovers from the overnight festival, he comes straight to the point.

"Marco, why don't you leave?"

"Chet my friend, I am pledged to your queen and your task. I will do as you say, and I will leave if you want."

"Has Axa pardoned you?"

"I don't know."

"You must ask her. Then we can move on, confident in the blessing of the spirits."

"Now that Axa has told the queens, I need to be pardoned by the whole nation."

"You should start with her. You released her chains on the ship and she spared you for stealing grain. Why not ask Luca for help? You are two sides of the same brooch - the gods flipped you in the air, and they could flip you back again." Chet's imagery sums up the changing fortunes and truces of these two renegades.

"A pardon for my part in slavery is my problem. Luca has enough to worry about."

"Marco, there are many stories of wounds being healed. A few moons ago, as a special guest you saw the Chicora and the Calusa tribes heal their wounds in ritual battle. Major arguments are resolved without miserable death, because the poisoned arrow-tips are cut off."

Marco huffs and turns to his tormentor. "As you say, mock fighting explains the lack of injuries in the buried bones of the past. We Spanish can only wish for a warless life back in Spain, without deadly feuds."

Marco sits like a scolded child. Trust is staying in the shadows, under rocks, or behind trees - uncertain how to proceed. Chet can point the way, but with this strange truce of Axa and Marco, they will have to sort out their differences in their own time.

Outside Axa's tepee, the whole Santee group squat in a circle as she explains that only she, Marco, and Luca will seek out the new Spanish colony - leaving the others to return home. Immediately Jay and Chet insist on coming, and she accepts their demands.

Then Marco speaks about a possible setback. "Axa, their leader Governor Toledo is known for fairness. However, they will also include Captain Cadiz, to whom I owe my life."

"How so?" Axa flicks an eyebrow.

Marco is embarrassed, as his divided faith and debts are nakedly exposed. Axa need not remind the group that she spared him from the death sentence for stealing grain – so he owes his life to her too.

"Er... he, er, spared me from the gallows for stealing his knife."

Axa leaves the squirming Marco to absorb the scorn of the others and then she changes the subject - warning them about the role of the coastal tribes.

"The Calusa have been helping the Spanish, so we alone must do the bidding of the gathering. We don't have to explain how we will make the colony fail."

Marco then talks out of turn... "Axa, how will we make it...?" Chet is squatting next to him and digs him in the ribs with his elbow. Marco grunts and looks at Luca for a reason – but gets a blank look.

Seeing their unease, Axa nods at each in turn.

"One step at a time, my braves, one step at a time."

Each man nods in turn and Marco accepts this isn't the time for detailed planning, or probing their chances of success.

She stands up, patting them each on the shoulder, and they take this as a hint to go about their business.

Axa stares at a grain of sand. How can they dislodge a clever and zealous foreign camp, from right under the noses of a local clan? They will need Marco's knowledge of Spanish ways, and her expertise on the Africans. Luca knows both the Calusa and this voyage in particular. That gives them a head start.

"Luca," Axa suggests, as he is about to walk away, "as matter of courtesy you must visit the Calusa queen. They know you, so you can explain why the Spanish aren't welcome in this land." She continues, looking him in the eye but smiling slightly. "Say *we* are chosen to tell them because I was a captive, Marco is a Spanish runaway, and you are a spy."

Luca scowls slightly.

"Of course, you will be vital if any Calusa scouts need to be put off, and you still need to tell them about your many friends... those lost at sea with the aborted Spanish voyage last spring."

"Thank you Queen Axa."

She nurtures the value of his many roles with different tribes... sailor, Calusa, and now Santee. His usual blank face has returned, but he fidgets.

"Luca, are you staying or going?" Axa sees a child hiding something, buffeted by feelings of loneliness and celebrity. He has a soul that cannot be trusted, because it cannot even trust itself.

OPTIONS

Chet's fingers feel fat from moulding a mixture of berries and dried meat that is beginning to crumble. It isn't normal to be hostile to newcomers. The legends of tolerance and trade always end well, and as the great eagle knows, they all rely on shared ideas and shared bloodlines.

He goes outside and gazes thoughtfully at Luca. No other brave has done so much in such a short life - courting popularity, mimicking and joking, or spurting out his stories with little offer. Deeper down though, he is a solitary person who might wander off at any time, possibly never to return.

"Chet, you're very quiet." Jay says, as he walks past her tepee.

"I was thinking about our task," he happily opens up about his concerns. "We will need the power of the hummingbirds, so we can be fearless defenders of our territory. With trust in each other, we can be many times stronger than our size would suggest."

"Don't talk in riddles. Now say what you mean."

"It's Marco and Luca. Marco has promised his loyalty to Axa, and Luca is, after all, one of us."

"And..."

"Well, he's been hurt by being taken by the Spanish."

"Chet you great bear, there's nothing we can do but trust in him. Axa has chosen him for our task, and he knows the swamps better than any of us."

They load up the last few things for the journey to the sea, and Chet seizes an opportunity to quiz Luca about the coastal forces.

"Luca, Sir. Tell me about our spirit guides?"

"Chet, you are famous for your knowledge of these

things. There's nothing I can teach you."

"My expertise is with the bear as protector, and the deer as a sign of wealth. I know the coyote is a trickster, but none of these tracks will be seen where we are going. I'm not sure if we will see the wise owl... as our departed leaders, or the eagle... carrier of our prayers?"

"Instead, you will see the crane, giving distant sight, and the death-defying turtle might give us grit."

Jay hears the young men showing off and decides to get them to focus on final packing. "My dear Chicoran wizard, the cricket may show with its welcome music, or the dragonfly as the messenger."

She has stopped Luca and Chet in their tracks and seizes the moment... "Come on you students of sorcery. Save your breath and your spirit skills. We will certainly need them soon."

In due course, they set off for the Spanish camp, travelling fast and light. Chet has explained that they won't need tepees or sleds, and they will use lean-to shelters for their brief rests. The most direct route across the valleys isn't suited to riding, but they can use some of the dogs and horses as pack animals.

After a few days crossing the foothills, they pass through the land of fire. Chet harks back to myths about trees springing miraculously from the sandy soils, after forest-fires sweep through. Then a firebird from the Overworld rises from the ashes, flaps its enormous wings, and the forest regrows in the spring.

"Are there signs in this forest?" Jay asks Chet, as they trek steadily towards the sea. "I see the nuthatch feeding on pine seeds here, with the warbler eating berries over there. The bluebird and the woodpecker call us, but what does it all mean?"

"Jay, my Princess," Chet adjusts his necklace, "it is the armadillo and the possum that have caught my eye."

"Don't call me Princess. Now why do you notice them? Do they favour treachery or trickery? Are they with the snake or the spider?"

"No. They just taste better."

Turning in a flash, she clouts him on the ear with her arrow pouch, and she tries to knock him to the ground. He steps over her futile trips, before collapsing as if treading in a trap and dragging her on top of him.

"You two, stop behaving like grasshoppers," Luca barks. You are supposed to be the leaders and all around there are enemies." He points into the dense forest ahead, before pushing them onwards. "Now let's get back on track."

The trek stretches out through the forest for several more days, passing moist soils where hardwood trees overtake the pines. During a morning ritual, Axa wishes that Ona were there to help find a brilliant idea - but she can only see her in dreams. The old way with newcomers is to be open and unarmed. Treachery or brutality are repaid in kind, but the advice from the gathering is clear... the newcomers aren't welcome. Axa, Marco, and Luca can't give this message to the Spanish face to face because they are all runaways from that tribe.

"Chet could tell them to leave," she muses aloud over tea and a biscuit.

Luca and Marco are loitering on their haunches nearby, waiting patiently for Axa to ask about the task.

"Axa," Luca bounces forwards, "they have no queens here and their priests twist the words of their prophet. Their saviour says they should love God first, which they do, and then love thy neighbour, which they do not." He pauses, as if he has seen the abyss at the end of the world. "They have a treaty with the Portuguese, but they fight all the northern sailors. They will try and convert us to their beliefs and if we reject them, they will use it as an excuse to use and enslave us."

"Axa," Marco also has his ideas rehearsed and ready, "they want to find treasure and spread the word of their god. Their brains are washed with greed, power and duty. They have already used brutality and treachery to destroy the Taino clans of Dominica and the Aztec - and they will have pistols, muskets, and cross-bows."

"What use are they against our faster bows?" Axa says. This doesn't need an answer, because it is now widely known that the explosive pipes and cross-bows are too slow to reload, and not accurate. They would only be of use in battle in large numbers, and then only in defence.

There is a long silence, as the purpose of the Spanish voyage sinks in, and there seems no chance of meeting minds in the old way.

"I will not allow treachery," she flicks her plaits. "To offer peace and then brutality will lead to a cruel circle of distrust and revenge. I will ask the spider."

Luca's smiling face shows she is referring to trickery, and he gives Marco a brotherly pat on the back, a big wink, and sets about the morning chores. Marco knows his place and sets about his own chores too, but with his mind full of espionage.

Jay stays briefly to give Axa an update on the fitness of the pack-horses and dogs, and the stories from the forward scouting. From words on the wind, the colony is taking shape at an alarming rate.

CURSE

Near the new colony, Governor Toledo and Captain Cadiz are discussing events over dinner, aboard one of the two remaining ships. Pedro, the captain of the other ship, joins them.

"There is a curse this quest to find a seaway to Asia," Toledo muses. "Two years ago the King sent Captain Gomez to chart the coast south from Labrador, and he found nothing."

He takes a long drag on his cigar.

"And there is a curse on this enterprise in particular. The return from the reconnaissance last spring saw one ship sunk on the open ocean. Now another vessel has already been stranded on a sandbank. Damn luck, that happened weeks before we even started the Catholic Mission."

Cadiz looks carefully at him. This aging and an ailing servant of the king of Spain has spent a lifetime extending the king's reach into the New World. Now he is increasingly doubtful about whether it has been a life well spent.

"That was just bad luck," Cadiz suggests. "But the heroism of the slaves and the emergence of a slave leader may be more important." He avoids eye contact, and dodges the question of whether having slave leaders is a good or a bad thing.

"I agree Sir," Pedro nods. "For better or worse, we have made a new contract with the Africans and the Indians." Pedro has the boastful appearance of a conquistador from his boots to his beard - with breeches, belt, and snug-fitting doublet all speaking of authority. He has rich, chestnut face hair compared to Toledo's silver beard, and the tiger-striped beard sported by Cadiz.

"Captain Pedro," Toledo probes the comment about the shipwreck, "What do you mean by a 'new contract'?"

"Sir," Pedro starts in a sombre tone, "I can see it in the eyes of my men. The Africans and the Calusa distinguished themselves during the scuttling of that ship. If a man pulls you from alligator infested waters - well, sailors don't forget that kind of thing."

"I see," Toledo sips a large glass of port. "The contract in Dominica is simple. If you are African, you work or you die. Indeed many die from work, and there have been rebellions by those who would rather die trying to escape. That brutal system is unlikely to make a success of this Mission, not least because the Africans will be hard to replace."

"Governor," Pedro adds, "If I learnt anything from my Indian friend, Luca de Chicora, it is that Indians don't use captivity. They believe in reincarnation, and they assume any man or woman would rather take their chances in the next life, than suffer captivity in this one."

"Your 'friend'." Cadiz exclaims. "As you know, that famous Indian was my protégé and he has escaped from this very expedition. He didn't drown in the shipwreck but got ashore, and we have been here for weeks with no sign of him."

"Enough," Toledo instructs. He is old and weak in body, but he is still the king's senior representative here. "I don't believe in reincarnation, but in the will of God. On behalf of the king, I will strike a new deal with the Indians and Africans. The people from this land of giants will be treated with honesty, and the Africans will be treated with respect. Now fetch the African leader... the man who led the evacuation at the shipwreck."

Soldiers are immediately dispatched to bring him to the dinner and Cadiz takes the opportunity to raise the matter of his own ambitions - to find natural resources in this new land.

"Governor and Cousin Pedro." Cadiz doffs his head to both Toledo and Pedro, "With respect, you may recall the banishment of my boson, Marco de Serena, those seven or eight months ago. No doubt he set off to find that high-value slave girl. I believe he intends to use her to help find gold, as the Ashanti can smell it in the wilderness. There are rumours she has settled among the Santee tribe who live up-river from here."

"I have heard that rumour too," Toledo grumbles. "Dominica is awash with spies and rumours. Never mind African queens. More importantly we have found common ground on working with the Indian and the African leadership."

After a short time, four soldiers push a reluctant giant into the room, with chains round his ankles and his wrists. It's clear he is expecting to be punished, as no African has ever set foot in the captain's quarters, which are steeped in the history of the Spanish navy and the saga of global exploitation. Trophies of a fair trade with African, East Indian and Asian networks sit next to trophies of bloody wars with other European tribes.

"Release his chains," Toledo orders.

The soldiers on either side do this, while two others stand nearby with hands on swords. In the crowded space, only the African has to bow his head below the upper deck.

"God be with you," Toledo uses the Ashanti tongue. "I know your name is Kofi, but I want to give you a Spanish name."

"Sir, I don't need a Spanish name to die. My name is Kofi Tutu Osei," he replies in Spanish. Finding a space for his head between the beams, he stands his full height.

His glistening teeth are visible but a shadow is cast across his eyes, which stare out of the windows to the swamps beyond. He rubs the calluses on his wrists caused by the cuffs, and speaks in perfect Spanish.

"You will have to kill me in cold blood."

"Lord be praised. God would never pardon such a thing," Toledo concedes the moral ground, and he concedes to speaking in Spanish. "Your personal heroism and the courage of your colleagues saved many Spanish lives during the shipwreck." He lets the silence speak for itself and defuses the threat of violence.

Kofi tips his head forward staring at Toledo, and speaks quietly in a creole of Spanish and Ashanti.

"We are in this together. If we have to get out of here together, then so be it."

Toledo sits back and nods gently, before proposing a deal to release their handcuffs in the daytime. Thinking aloud, he explains that this will increase their work-rate without conceding too much control. If it works, then more concessions can be made.

Kofi's hands and feet are unchained and he is allowed to leave – with only Cadiz muttering curses. He goes to the council that has formed among the Africans and tells them about Toledo's concessions. The group is a mixture of young men and women from a number of the West African cultures, but Kofi is able to address them using a common tongue and signs.

"The Spanish are making us an offer of better treatment. We all want freedom, but not at any cost. Many of us came here on the same ships many moons ago, and we have kept our ancient and shared Akan gods."

One of Kofi's female cousins sees that he has no ankle chains and could escape if he wanted.

"Brothers and sisters, these lower gods will assist each of us here on Earth. For all of us, they get their power from the same supreme creator."

"Cousin," Kofi continues, with all the others listening intently, "we have priestesses among us who can act as go-betweens to the gods and for our cause. If we practice daily prayer and pour potions each morning as an offering to the ancestors, we will succeed."

"Prince Kofi," another woman in the group leans forward, "we know our distant ancestors are buried under this land as much as our homeland."

There is general nodding and the group as a whole decide to wait for their chance of freedom.

RENDEZVOUS

Axa listens to stories from local scouts who are being carefully checked by Chet and Jay. It's clear that the colony itself is struggling with the wildness of the coast, but with the help of the Calusa the shipwreck hasn't been a total disaster. Only a few souls were lost, and the rest of the crew managed to escape from the sea onto the other two ships. They finally found a sheltered anchorage and started clearing a part of the forest where the land rises above the swamps.

She and the others are closing in, but not before meeting up with some Santee scouts to pick up supplies and clothing. Her group had packed for a gathering, with all the ceremony that goes with that great event, and now they need to thwart the Catholic Mission. They will also need to carry everything they need, as the wetlands ahead aren't suited to horses or dogs.

"How is Ona?" Axa asks the Santee scouts as they get to the meeting place.

"Ask her yourself," Kuruk replies, riding out from behind some rocks - leading Ona on her horse.

Without much of a head start, Kuruk has used the valley trails to get to the Santee's summer villages, and then he has ridden with Ona to the rendezvous. Despite the high feeling of the moment, Axa has a fleeting and frightening thought - what if Kuruk and Ona were cast-outs or bandits after their food? Worse still, what if they were bounty hunters... come to kill them for the prices on their heads? Devil Fear, if horses are from the Underworld, what havoc might they cause among a people who have settled the land without them? The new painting she had seen in the caves before the bear attack flashed into her mind, with beast and man as one animal -

the Overworld must have fixed the ancient horses of this land into the rocks for a reason?

"Axa," Ona shouts, "come here and let me touch you." She is unable to contain her joy, as she leaps off her horse. Her nimbleness belies her slight blindness, and Axa is stunned as Ona smothers her in her arms.

"Kuruk you should not have done this," Axa sobs, still clutching Ona like the soft toys of her childhood.

"Princess Axa, I was only obeying my new queen."

With that, Chet pulls Kuruk off his horse and gives him a bear hug, swinging him about like a rag doll.

"Put me down. This is no way to treat a future Santee prince," Kuruk grunts in embarrassment.

Jay finally manages to prise her mother and Axa apart, whereupon she is squashed in their gripping embrace.

Everybody sits down cross-legged, while the rest of the scouts become lookouts or tend to the horses and dogs. Axa and Ona are joined at the hip but the others have enough space to exchange warm smiles and laughter. After absorbing the joy of being reunited, Axa decides to come straight to the point.

"This is a task for runaways, not Santee queens and Pensacola princes" She looks at Kuruk wide-eyed and unblinking.

Kuruk looks back at her, mouthing silently 'I will deal with the Spanish colony. Leave it to me.'

Chet shakes his head and looks at Kuruk with raised eyebrows. He straightens his body, leans back and splays his hands low in front of him... 'Back off' is the clear message.

Ona jumps into the awkward space, "What about the Calusa?" easing Kuruk's fervour and focussing on the unknown issues.

Luca interrupts out of turn, but with a cheeky smile.

"The Calusa are swept by hurricanes every summer, so even they don't know what they are up to."

"There's some truth in that," Axa adds more soberly. "The advice of the gathering is to deter the Spanish garrison. The spider tells me they will be deterred if the colony isn't workable."

Marco then gives his thoughts, as the expert on Spanish plans. "The colony depends on African labour, so they will be deterred if we free the Africans." It's a clear issue, but this puts the matter beyond doubt.

Kuruk looks at Axa, thinking how young their love is and how jealous he feels that she might see her African fiancée again. Is this why she wants to go to the colony without him? They all get up for a stretch and Axa leaves Ona with Jay to refresh their bonds, while she goes to Kuruk.

"I've missed you Kuruk."

"It's only been a quarter moon."

"In another three quarters of the moon we can be married. Now you must take Ona back home."

"In case you don't come back?"

"My love, I won't take any chances. You know the spirits are with us. I mean they are with you and me, as a union. I love you and until now I have only known men I have been arranged to marry, by my mother."

"Axa, I say Chet and Jay should go back with Ona, and I should come with you."

"Kuruk, I just can't think straight with you around." She heaves a sigh… loving him too much to endanger him on this personal adventure. "I promise you… ." She stops as she notices his eyes reddening, with wells gathering in his bottom eyelids. One big tear slips down a long, black eyelash.

"You promise," Kuruk growls. Her mind is made up for whatever reason, and there is no use trying to change it.

They hug in silence and he eventually puts her down, before walking off alone, hunched, and kicking at flies.

Axa finds Ona and Jay arguing as if they had never been apart.

"Take great care Jay," Ona rubs her hands together. "Other tribes have different values to us. Not bad, just different."

"Like you took care of yourself on your walkabout, visiting the far-off Aztec and the Inuit." Jay responds, as if still a surly teenager.

Ona takes a breath and is about to rebuke Jay, but Axa interrupts. She asks Ona to tell everybody what will happen next, so nobody will doubt the wisdom and future success of the idea. Prince Kuruk is tending the horses – too proud or heartbroken to hear the plan in an open forum, but Ona announces that he will take her back while the others continue as planned.

The groups go their separate ways and Axa feels her heart pulled up into her chest - towards her duty; and then down into her belly – towards her new love. To help her focus on her duty she invites demons into her thoughts, carrying memories of the evil of captivity.

Come now demons and turn into Spanish sailors. They don't come - her demons never obey her orders. Nevertheless, the effort at least distracts her long enough for Kuruk and Ona to vanish into the forest with all the horses and dogs, along with the rest of the scouts that came to the rendezvous.

CLOWNS

They travel another day until they hear seagulls and see flocks of other seabirds on the far horizon. Chet's interest becomes too much for him, and stopping for a rest he makes a proposal.

"Axa, we are now so near we can hear the colony, if not smell it. The thud of fence-posts being hammered is mixed with the far-off thunder of ocean storms, and I'm ready to take a closer look."

"Thank you Chet, but you may be gone a long time." She cups her tea in her hands and draws the scent into her nostrils. "With the wind on our backs this morning you would need to go right round to the seaward side. In these swamps that might take half a day, and by that time the fickle wind could go round too, so they would still smell you first."

"My queen," Chet persists, "the sea has spent the night sucking the air off the land, and soon it will spend the day blowing it back ashore."

She notes that he's been learning from Luca how this strange place needs different skills to the foothills. Leafy hardwood forests grow out of the floodplains and the yearly floods have built up the muddy soils alongside the rivers and lakes. Gum, oak, and cypress trees grow gnarled knees and fluted trunks, playing tricks on Axa's mind, and conjuring up gruesome tree-men with twisted faces.

From her own time in these swamps, she knows the colony will have sprouted on the first piece of raised land that they found. Around this island, chiefly on the far, seaward side, would be brackish swamps. She calls upon memories of a dreamy place, where orchids grow in water traps among the cypress branches. Bees dance among the tupelo trees that rule the forest – with chestnut and walnut jostling for space. Then the broad, droopy leaves of the pawpaw take the last of the light before it reaches the swamp.

"Chet," Axa asks in a sombre tone, "I know you have joked with the others about the powers here... but it's all a bit... well... sinister." She looks around at the strange and peaceful beauty of a forest that floats on a mirror of black glass.

"Indeed Axa," Chet responds, slowly surveying the scene. "This place is other-worldly and half asleep. Many slow-moving creatures like giant snails and millipedes live off the rotting carpet around us. The mushrooms and lichen on the decaying logs just ignore the seasons. I would rather be a bird here, and nest among the orchids."

He looks up into the canopy as if in a dream, and to his utter astonishment, among those orchids is a pair of blue eyes.

"What in hell's gate are you doing here?" Chet muffles a shout.

"One false move and you're dead," Jay whispers from a place beyond the imposter. She had sensed something, and she is now behind the stalking creature with bow and arrow, poised to unleash death.

"Jay, don't shoot. It's Inca," Chet pleads.

Inca is perched high up in the canopy. He has curled his bony limbs into a nest formed by the swirling arms of a great cypress tree. Perhaps he managed to follow the Santee scouts to their rendezvous with Axa's group. Then he must have followed these five to this place, undetected by any of them.

"Come down here my little hunter friend," Marco laughs. "You have flown in under the nose of Chet, my own tutor in the art of stalking."

"Under the noses of all of us," Luca adds. He can tell that Jay and Axa don't see the funny side of Inca following them so easily.

"You are lucky I didn't pin you to that tree," Jay interjects.

"You cheeky little shape-shifter," Chet reaches up to help Inca down. "You are a tadpole, with magical powers to change how you look." His joke excuses everyone's failure to notice the intruder.

"Come here you clown," Axa refers to the spirit of good luck. "I think I have a task for you."

Is Ona somehow behind Inca's appearance? She and Kuruk may have brought him at least as far as the rendezvous. Axa doesn't care but she will use this boy's magic. If it is Ona or Kuruk's doing, then their souls and guile are with him too.

Inca slithers down to join the group, who are scowling or smiling at him in equal measure. Soon they set off on high alert, and can clearly hear the noise of building-work blowing on the wind - now increasingly coming off the sea.

There are one or two encounters with Calusa scouts, but they aren't interested in this Santee hunting party, even with its unusual mix. They accept that Axa, Marco, and Luca all have their own reasons for being there, but Jay does raise a few eyebrows, not least because she is such a beautiful princess. However, she has Chet as a chaperone and given Axa's three spirals, this all suggests their group should enjoy some respect, whatever their reasons for coming to the lowlands.

From Axa's point of view, they should not lie to the Calusa about deterring the Catholic Mission. On the other hand, they need not be fully updated either - unless their queen specifically asks for more facts.

Even with the luck of the sea-wind allowing them to stalk from inland, the going is more and more swampy. The sound of chopping, sawing, and banging-in posts fills the breeze as Axa sucks in the smells of working horses and men that are mixed in with the salty air. The new Spanish colony is no more than a shout away, but it must be on an island if this swamp is anything to go by.

She, Marco, and Luca have all crossed similar wetlands as runaways, so to be doing it again is testing their steadfastness to their task.

"Axa," Luca whispers as he comes near to her at a vantage point, "we could be surrounded and not even know it."

Their eyes scan a forest so dense that they can only see between the nearest trees to the next tree, or maybe see the one beyond. Axa holds up her hand until everyone stops moving and then she listens and sniffs the air. After a few moments, she responds to Luca's point.

"We aren't surrounded unless there are spirits in these muddy shallows."

"The Calusa legends," Luca eventually adds, "say their ancestors lost their fur while living here. They were half-submerged and half fish. They think all people sprung from those first Calusa swamp-women."

"My dear Catfish," Axa replies, "you have a mouth wide enough to swallow a horse." She looks at him, and her eyes twinkle but her face is blank. "Now you move ahead, and don't make a splash."

They all spread out a little more as they wade through the black water. Each takes turn to make progress while the others stop on the driest patch of ground, or on a low-hanging bough. The giant roots of the trees spread out like a dancer's skirt. Many trees seem to have snake-like features from the vines climbing over them towards the light. Some enormous tree-roots have spread so far that they detach from the main trunk. Other trees have been so heavily covered in vines that the tree inside has died and rotted away - leaving the hollow, woven shell of vine branches.

A rhythm develops among the group, with one moving and five watching for an ambush. That is unless Inca needs a piggyback, in which case he is never far from Chet. Like a giant insect moving one limb at a time - almost as one creature - they creep towards the noise of the colony. When Chet's turn comes to move up from the back, Inca waits for his lift. The rhythm breaks. Nothing moves.

Chet has gone.

SETBACK

One by one everyone locates Inca with their eyes among the curtains of roots. One by one, Inca returns their stares, waves his hands about, and mouths in ever-increasing fear.

"He's not here."

"Behind you," Jay signs to him, waving a pointed finger.

Inca looks behind and all around, but there is no sign of Chet. Barely a ripple disturbs the large pond where he was standing a few moments earlier. Then a big eddy of oily liquid, laden with rotting plants from the pond bed, swells up just beyond Inca. A great fight is taking place in the shallows, but hidden from view under the churning surface. A huge, scaly tail flips out, then over and over again - a young alligator in a death spin.

"Everyone, stop it turning or it will rip his leg off," Luca shouts.

The whole group throw themselves headlong into the fight with the thrashing beast. Marco is nearest, quickly followed by Luca. They each leap on to a back leg, while Jay and Axa each grab a front leg. The tail still thrashes, but the twisting is stopped by the effort of lifting two people out of the water, and dragging two under the swirling soup.

Chet's limbs start to show, other than the leg in the jaws of the animal. Finally, his head bursts out of the greasy water gasping for air. Inca catches up with them, and he leaps onto the scaly, primeval head - plunging his knife between its eyes and banging it in with his club.

Slowly the alligator stops fighting and its great jaws loosen their grip on Chet's leg. He pulls free, and drags himself to a patch of sand among the giant roots. Jay releases her hold on the animal as it is now fading away, and she wades across to him. His leg has no open gashes, deep puncture wounds, or broken bones, because he twisted with the jaws as they span around.

Bless our luck, Axa prays, this beast isn't full-grown and the jaws are a clamp, rather than for ripping their prey. The others leave the beast to die, but Inca keeps banging the handle of the knife deeper into its skull.

"Inca, I think it's dead now," Luca shakes a fist. "You have cut its mind from its body. Well done."

"Chet, are you alright?" Marco rushes to him. "You gave him a good kick in the teeth."

"I'm fine," Chet manages to say, but winces as he tries to stand on the damaged leg. "I can hold my breath longer than any giant lizard."

"You can come back in the next life as the immortal terrapin," Axa teases. "Now we must expect a patrol from the colony."

They all switch their fear to another threat - the Spanish. Any salute to Chet's rescue will have to wait for another day. Spreading out again, they wait for a detachment but none comes.

After an hour of silence, Axa's thoughts return to their task and they move even closer to the colony. When they finally see the camp they are staggered by its size. The combined effort of men, women, and horses has turned the wilderness into a settlement where they have already put up many buildings. The three tribes of Spanish, Calusa, and African are settled into busy routines that belie the steamy heat, and the constant attack from mosquitos and leeches.

"Inca, I have a special job for you," Axa gestures across to him. "I want you to go to Dark Cloud, the leader of the Calusa here, and then get into the fortress."

With undoubting duty, Inca slips away and he is next seen running like a demented puppet out of the forest and into the clearing. From their view point, Axa and the rest can see a few muskets raised towards Inca, but he is among the Calusa group before much ado.

Soon he is taken to the structure in the centre and doesn't reappear for several hours. When he does, the soldiers scattered around the camp accept him and they ignore his silly antics and dancing. Axa decides it will be an extra night among the leeches before the rest of them attempt any access.

They take on a rota of keeping watch, eating, or sleeping for another silent, moonlit eternity. During that night, Jay is restless and goes to Axa.

"Axa, our men are haunted by fear. Luca and Marco mainly... but even Chet is catching their fever."

"What are they afraid of?" Axa has her own ideas, but wants to encourage Jay's thinking.

"Fear of the other. Fear of failure. Fear of the afterlife," Jay lists these deep-seated worries as if they are wounds on Chet's leg.

"How so, 'fear of the other'?"

"Not each other. They are all good friends now. These moons of travelling and this shared adventure have stuck them together. I mean fear of how their different cultures can find peace."

"Jay my dear, men are cursed with self-doubt. Before the beginning of the world, a ghost planted this seed in the first father - to be passed to all sons. They wonder if they are strong or clever enough to survive and protect their families. This breeds mistrust and rivalry, which dances and fights with the spirit of love. It is up to us to wash the doubt away and let love prevail."

"Great Axa, I too have doubted this quest."

"Princess," Axa cups Jay's cheeks in her hands, "I never doubt you. I am so sure of you. You must show Chet, Luca, and Marco that you are sure of them. Trust in them and they will trust in themselves. Fear will be a helpless ghost."

Axa closes her eyes... Trust in love. The Spanish, African, and Santee gods have the same message, and chaos has been forced into the shadows since the Dreamtime? No stories, art, or bones bear witness to brutality between First Peoples in this land.

Jay goes back to sentry duty, content with Axa's advice. She will bolster the men in the morning by telling them how sure she is that they will succeed, and a cycle of fear will be shunned. Axa on the other hand isn't so sure, despite her backing of Jay.

All her life she was taught to fear nothing, and she would be rewarded in the next life. Now there is a nagging doubt in her heart. Something in the wind says the balance is under threat - that the circle of life itself is being broken, and that this other world might one day eclipse their world altogether.

As she stares out into the ghostly, moon-soaked forest, the skirts of the trees swirl on a polished dancefloor. Images of her mother and Ona emerge in the mist and they come towards her.

"Mama and Ona, I hope you haven't come to talk about my love life." Axa mouths.

"Dearest Axa," her mother frowns. "Listen carefully. There is a shaman with the Spanish leader called a friar. He talks to their Creator, so Governor Toledo both fears and loves him. He's the secret of your success and he carries the hopes and dreams of this Catholic Mission - but he can be won over."

"Can this shaman be turned from their dream of paradise?" Axa asks the spectres. "This is the idea that misleads them so much."

"No," Ona says bluntly. "That dream is so fixed in their hearts that they cannot see any other afterlife. They cannot come back as eagles like we can. In the name of our ancestors, the friar can only be turned if we give him a trophy... something to show for his efforts with this voyage."

"What kind of trophy..." Axa asks desperately, "...a queen?"

Axa's mother is about to reply when an owl swoops across their path. Its talons are tucked back as it glides onto a hapless mouse, then they slip forward to spear it from behind. Hunter and prey lift into the night sky to join the bats, darting after the juiciest moths. Nature is at its busiest, when only the fastest or cleverest will feed, or be weaker for the next attempt.

Owls foretell bad luck, so what does this killing mean right here before her eyes? Must she herself be the trophy the Spanish need to take away... dead or alive? She shivers as if cold water was poured down her back, and watches the owl glide off into the night. Squinting to re-focus on the dream, the spirits of her mother and Ona have gone.

APPROACH

Through the mist next morning, Axa observes the colony waking and coming back to life. Inca's theatrical accounts are added together with her own view of the soldiers, Africans, and Calusa within the perimeter. There are a few comings and goings from the ships, but they can be watched easily from a safe distance.

Inca also describes the inner-workings of the leadership within the officer's quarters.

'The Calusa leader, Dark Cloud, has pow-wow with the Captains and the Chief,' Inca dances and chants. 'The Calusa want to learn to use the fire-pipe and the Spanish want the Calusa scouts to help them explore inland.' Then he does a weird dance with a clear but unlikely message. 'The African leader has pow-wow with the Spanish about their wrist-cuffs being removed at night, as well as during the day, while the Spanish want the Africans to work with the saws and axes.'

"He must be mistaken," Marco watches Inca's dance. "Captives don't negotiate with their captors."

Axa stays silent, but her wounded heart thumps in her chest and she struggles to keep the past nightmares at bay. Heart heal yourself. Bitterness is a risk to reasoning... keep an open mind.

"It's possible," Luca nods. "Toledo is a tortured man who often unburdened his soul to me over a glass of port. He hates this part of the trade triangle - the trade in people. On this trip, I also saw first-hand many soldiers and sailors being lifted from the water by Africans after the shipwreck. That kind of brotherhood can cross race, colour, and creed."

"Toledo spared me from the gallows," Marco adds, "but only in a conspiracy with Cadiz to put me in debt.

Luca, how is Governor Toledo's health?"

"He's a dead man walking," Luca uses the Chicoran saying, rather than Spanish. "I'm sorry. I mean he's about to die."

"What type of men..." Axa asks, "...are Cadiz and the other captain?" She waits, as neither Luca nor Marco wants to commit themselves. Luca is reluctant to talk about Cadiz and looks blankly at Marco.

"I will speak for Cadiz," Marco straightens. "This leopard cannot change his spots in a matter of months. Captain Cadiz is motivated by one thing - he wants enormous, life-long riches – but he will not bother with lost causes. At least he's not proud."

"Then I will speak for Captain Pedro," Luca says. "He's motivated by rank. This leopard will change his spots happily - from slaver to trader to statesman. Like Cadiz, he's not single-minded and will spin any outcome of this adventure to his advantage."

"Now," Axa looks at Luca, "tell me about the Calusa's stake in this Catholic Mission." Luca's reason being taken along with the Calusa braves not so long ago is still doubtful. Some clarity is needed.

"Axa, your escape and Marco's arrest belied a good contact between me, the Calusa, and the Spanish. It's true, the voyage found nowhere to come ashore and start building, but we agreed to help them chart the coast, trading this for ship-building skills."

"Thank you Luca. So, none of them are prepared to die here," Axa says. The others don't refute her and she pursues issues that are more spiritual. "What about the Spanish god?"

Marco is best placed to answer this, but he mumbles as he grudgingly searches his mind for memories of his former beliefs.

"My god is all-knowing, all powerful. Above all, people fear him. Their priest, the Dominican friar, will remind them that the purpose of this colony is to spread the word of God. If they are to leave without a fight we must yield something." He flattens his stomach. "It is my job to persuade him."

It crosses Luca's mind to explain about demonising the spirals – to pit one god against another. He has everybody looking at him for a moment, so he must not dither, but he stares blankly into the middle distance. No – this cannot be explained now – he will save that secret for another day, or maybe even another gathering. He changes the subject.

"Axa, what do you know about the African prince?"

"He will do as I say. That is all you need to know." She flicks her wristband. "Now let's talk about weapons and truces."

Axa leaves it to the others to volunteer what they know. Marco goes first.

"The muskets aren't accurate, but they can be used together to create a killing-zone at fifty paces. They will form three rows, and fire in volleys – defeating any frontal-attack with the shorter-range bow and arrow. They also have some crossbows, but they are even slower to reload. Pistols can be used at closer quarters – with swords and daggers for hand-to-hand fighting."

Axa notes Marco's outward willingness to support her cause, but will it continue once the killing begins? Luca is next.

"The Calusa group, as always, have their bows across their chests and carry about twenty arrows each. This gives hundreds of precise shots with a range of about thirty paces. The African group have axes and saws, but are severely hampered by their chains."

Axa doesn't need to say that the odds will be in favour of the Spanish in any battle, because many injuries will be meted out in the twenty paces before arrows can be used.

"None of this military advantage occurs by chance," Marco adds. "Pedro has spent many years as a slaver and a soldier. He also thinks of the sailors, who could come with more weapons soon after hearing shots."

Clearly, revolt would be worse than the truce. Even if the Calusa change sides and they attack the Spanish alongside the Africans, the soldiers will be able to hold out. This is unlikely to happen as the Spanish have much to offer the Calusa, while the Africans have nothing. Axa goes deeper into the matter of the outward truces.

"It's the mutual interests of the Calusa and the Spanish that makes this whole thing possible. Therefore, Marco and Luca, you will have to upset the balance."

Marco is already thinking along the same lines. "Somehow the Calusa need to be turned."

"More importantly," Luca adds, "the Spanish have to believe they have lost the Calusa's trust."

Jay takes up the reins of the budding plan. "Marco and Luca, you must find a reason. Then Chet and I can pass this to the Calusa - at just the same time as you two can explain the new facts to the Spanish leaders."

Axa is impressed that Jay has seen this chance, and she allows it to settle in the minds of the others. This will need the spirit of Anansi the spider to be working at her best and for the Santee cause, but the great gathering has spoken to this same end, so Anansi should be on their side.

"Luca, my friend," Marco lowers his voice, "what really happened to your Calusa friends on the trip back to Dominica? After all, they were Dark Cloud's cousins."

"You mean the big lie," Luca is reading Marco's mind. "The false story that my Calusa friends were lost at sea?"

"Dark Cloud should know what happened, however awful," Marco adds.

"That is too horrible," Luca mumbles in pain, as the last rites of his Calusa friends come back to haunt him.

"What happened to them? Were they tortured - or turned into slaves?"

Luca starts to shed tears but from frozen eyes.

"Fungus," he stutters, as if about to choke. "A scourge from the Underworld."

A long stillness waits for the doors of hell to open, but Jay interrupts.

"Ha. I will tell them how they died... about the invisible curse spread by contact with the sailors."

There is more silence and shared eye contact to see if any of them dissent - before a general nodding in agreement.

Axa's thoughts go to Ona's illness. This would also start a wild rumour when there is no proof, but this story of disease might be true. If the disease did travel with the Spanish, and the First Peoples have no answer to it, this could be the catastrophe of her very worst nightmares.

For now, they need to focus on the task, so she breaks the uncomfortable pause.

"We will go into the colony soon. I will explain the plan after you have made peace with your gods. We will all be risking everything, and anything could happen."

LEGACY

The others spread out but Jay moves closer. She sees right through Axa's self-confident shell, because she also walks a tightrope between pride and doubt. Like Axa, she has all the benefits that royal blood brings, but she has also been made to feel worthless and meagre at one time or another. Now Jay has the confidence of the woman who has found the weakness in the enemy... the lie that the Calusa adventurers were lost at sea.

Jay speaks gently. "You do not have to do this. The Kristianos are our problem."

"I am not afraid of the abyss."

"Axa of the Ashanti, you came from nowhere, and deep down you were frightened before Mama gave you her love."

Jay has found more solid footing, while Axa is thigh-deep in black water, and allows herself to slouch as the weight of leading the task is shared with the younger Santee princess. She takes Jay by the wrists and looks up into her eyes.

"We are all frightened of failure. It's only love that makes us face that possibility every day, and then laugh it off into the shadows. Neither failure, nor our other fears, come to us in obvious clothing. They are all shape-shifters, sometimes masked as friends. Love can turn to jealousy, or failure can fall from pride. All our feelings, good and bad, can cut both ways."

Jay casts her eyes around for a hiding place before responding, "Sometimes I too want to be in the shadows, looking at those in the sunlight."

"Jay, you and I must love the shadows too, but not be afraid of our own shadows. None of us are here for long in this form. Some of us are only human in this life so our souls can choose their calling in the next life. This body can be a climbing ladder or a slippery pole between the Underworld and Overworld."

Jay stops fidgeting and pulls Axa onto a giant root where they can sit together, but warily facing opposite ways.

"My body," Jay says, "feels like a dream-catcher, spinning in the wind. Love, hate, love, hate... as the two faces of the wicker disc take turns to catch the light."

"Yes, but notice how the feathers hanging within the dream-catcher still find their own way. We must be like them, and find our own way. Then maybe we can serve our family, our clan, and our tribe when difficult choices have to be made."

"Axa, I will face these choices, and I will learn from them. The harder the choices, the more I will learn. I welcome the shape-shifters, whether in the shadows, the moonlight, or the sunlight."

Axa wants to ask what Jay would do if she saw the shape-shifters in her own mirror-image. What if they show when she washes her face in a bowl, or she checks her makeup in a polished shell? Instead, a well of pride fills in Axa's heart, hearing Jay's attitude to making hard choices... then the well empties into tears.

"Axa, have I upset you?"

"No, no." Axa mumbles. "It is just we have so much in common. My life was so like yours. Then my first baby miscarried. A little girl, the midwife said. Soon after that, the slave traders came and we had to escape to the mountains."

Jay had only seen Axa cry once before, and she awkwardly puts arms around her, as she had done at the gathering. Axa sobs and laughs, and sobs again.

"Princess Jay of the Santee, you already have two

beautiful daughters and I may never get that chance. Tell me what it feels like... to have children."

"Don't say that. You say you have a fiancé on the ships, and Kuruk waits for you too."

"Sister, I wish it could be true, but Ona and my mother told me in a dream that I will be taken back, dead or alive."

"Nonsense. Curse those dreams. I will not allow it."

"I said the same about my first husband. I would not let the Arabs take him. They did, and he was killed trying to escape. The rest of us fled, and were adopted by another tribe. I never saw my mother again... running away for many moons looking for her, time and again, while my surviving family always took me back. Another prince was found for me, but in time we were all captured anyway."

"My sister," Jay swings off the seating place, grips Axa by the shoulders, and pushes her up straight. "You must promise me you will not give yourself up. You are part of our destiny now. You will be a queen and a mother in our land."

Laughing and weeping mix together, as Axa shakes her head, wipes her face and pulls Jay to her this time.

"I promise I will not give up without a fight. You must promise to do just what I say."

Jay laughs under Axa's embrace.

"Agreed. As All-Seeing Eye is my witness."

AMBITION

"Marco, my friend," Luca asks tongue in cheek, as they lie a few paces apart, "who are you praying to?"

"It doesn't matter. All our gods want us to find peace. I just need to remind the friar that his god wants it too – then he can persuade the others."

"I prayed that both my gods talk to each other. I don't know how they will decide who goes to paradise, or who becomes a coyote...but they are gods after all. I will leave it to them."

Luca's chest sags, slowly exhaling the stale air from deep in his lungs, and from fatigue at being so many things to so many people. The years of courting popularity among such different tribes have left him with nothing left of himself, whoever that was before he was cast out as a boy.

Axa signals for everyone to close in on her and goes over the plan in detail. Using a stick, she sketches the colony in the sand with a large circle showing the clearing, and a smaller funnel-shape in the middle showing the fort. This is an open courtyard narrowing to an enclosed cabin.

"Any attack at first-light has the cover of the morning mist... but would have the sun in its eyes in the entrance. The funnel itself is about fifty paces long. God help them, as soon as warriors get through the wide entrance they will be within range and shot to pieces by rows of muskets defending the cabin." She swallows hard at the thought of the impending bloodshed.

She points at the others with the stick - each in turn - and fixes them in an unblinking, fiery gaze. Such is her self-belief that none of them doubts for a second that her plan is their destiny.

"Chet and Jay, you will go to Dark Cloud with your terrible story." She points them to the Calusa's place in her sketch, outside the fort. "Marco and Luca, you go to the Spanish leaders and the friar in the cabin. I will go to the Africans to keep them calm. If everything goes according to plan, I have a special role for them."

This leaves no one to deal with the twenty or so Spanish soldiers around the fort, or the sailors who are still with the other two ships. She is gambling that the soldiers will not shoot without orders, and the sailors will not come from the ships without a clear signal.

Marco adds his expertise. "The fort and cabin are a tried-and-trusted design, intended for defence. In a revolt, the high, spiked walls will channel any assault towards the only entrance and apertures at the cabin."

Axa sniffs. "Why does a message of 'love thy neighbour' need such defence? It is their prophet's second commandment, after loving god, so the Spanish must think we are brutal people."

She does one last check. The Calusa and African groups are taking their morning breaks in the open, relaxing between the fortress and the edge of the clearing, and twenty-four soldiers are spread out in twos and threes at key points, with two sergeants who can report to Pedro if necessary.

Some soldiers are catching up on sleep from night-watch duties, and some of the Calusa and African women are singing back-and-forth in a game. There are comings and goings from the ships and those harvesting the forest, while the soldiers keep watch. They are relaxed despite the hateful compromises that make it all possible.

Axa's group fiddle nervously with their disguises - each dressed to mix easily with their targets. Marco and Luca have dusted off their Spanish clothes and Jay is dressed as a boy. Axa tries to look like a woman from the African working party, and blocks out her terrible voyage from her mind.

While Inca performs a particularly crazy routine to distract the soldiers, they all creep into place around the edge of the clearing.

Chet and Jay get as close as possible to the twenty or so Calusa, who are eating biscuits and drinking tea. Axa takes up her place near to the African working party - about thirty strong, in ankle cuffs and chains. Marco and Luca post themselves covertly near the fortress, where Inca's stories say that Toledo is bed-bound and very weak.

Upon Axa's woodpecker signal, they all walk calmly into the clearing. Her whole plan depends on the soldiers withdrawing to the centre if they become alarmed, and forming a single body of men. They are well-trained, and even in this calm and absent-minded state they can become a fearsome force in seconds.

Chet and Jay make first contact with the Calusa as planned. Dark Cloud, their leader, is as brooding and compelling as his name suggests. His high bunch of hair is fuller than the others and he is longer in the limb and face. Typically, his skin is gleaming and youthful, but his sombre look makes him look much older than his twenty-five summers.

"Dark Cloud, of the Calusa," Chet bows low. Jay is on hand if the Calusa braves are startled. Chet holds the formal bow longer than normal. "I am Chet of the Santee, and this is Princess Jay. In the name of the Three Spirals we come in peace."

Dark Cloud gets up slowly from his haunches and the two braves next to him rise in slightly wary poses.

"Greetings Princess and Chet," Dark Cloud opens

his palms. "I know who you are, and we have been expecting you ever since you sent that clown Inca to spy on the Spanish. Chet, are you limping?"

"My leg is fine, thank you."

"So why do you dress like Calusa." Dark Cloud can see that Chet is edgy, but continues... "Do the Spanish know you are here?" He gestures for them all to resume sitting on their haunches.

"The Spanish do know we are here," Chet replies. "At least their leaders do. Your friend Luca and the Spaniard, Marco, are with them, explaining our visit. Pardon me, but we must come to the point... the soldiers are already looking this way."

"Dark Cloud," Jay jumps in, "we plead to your wisdom. There is great danger from an invisible spirit brought by the Spanish. Your cousins have already died of it." She pauses and states the rest of the shocking news coldly and clearly. "They were NOT lost at sea as you have been told."

Dark Cloud freezes, stunned both by Jay's startling green-eyed stare and by this astonishing, gut-wrenching news. His blood-brothers and many friends were lost with the explorers earlier in the year and the grieving is still fresh in his heart. To be misled about them is to have the ground ripped from under his feet and all their ghosts stare at him from a corrupt limbo.

Chet sees the Spanish coming over and hunches his huge frame meekly, turning his back on the two soldiers making their way towards them. "You must choose who to trust."

"Stay where you are." Dark Cloud stands up and shouts at the guards in competent Spanish.

He holds up his palm to face them and uses his other hand to gesture for the others to remain low. The soldiers stop in their tracks about thirty paces away, knowing that any closer and they will be in range of an arrow. Often, the Calusa show-off to the Spanish by arming themselves instantly and arrowing rabbits as they bolt. It is good-humoured, but the message is simple - we are so much quicker than you.

For the soldiers, arrows are whispering death. They will be stuck in their necks and legs before they even hear their whining song, and they would be put out of action before they see more arrows being launched from a rolling Calusa brave.

Behind the soldiers, more trouble is brewing among the Africans. Axa goes to them at the same time as Chet and Jay make contact with the Calusa, but they are unable to muffle their amazement. The sight of a healthy and long-lost Ashanti queen is too much.

"Prince Kofi, greetings," she winks.

Kofi chokes on his bread, spooking the nearest sentries, and the sergeants shout orders from near the fortress because multiple threats are emerging.

How will the soldiers react? Axa's heart grips itself for several beats, dreading the terrible noise of shots ringing out and the sight of bloody flesh bursting apart. Bless the spirals, the sergeant's orders are to withdraw and not to fire on anybody. The guards all jog to the centre, nervously checking that nobody is chasing them, and they vanish behind the fences in front of the little cabin.

For a few seconds there is a fusillade of shouted orders and a cloud of dust billows out, before silence. Inca is swept up in the retreat but thrown out from the funnel along with the dust, before running straight into Axa's warm, motherly embrace.

GAMBIT

By now, Marco and Luca are risking their lives inside the cabin itself. At the same time as the others sprang their surprise, they had performed their trick. Luca had walked straight up to a soldier with Marco as his prisoner, holding the pistol pushed into the Spaniard's back and ordering him forward, arms raised.

"Take this fugitive to the Governor." he had shouted to the startled guard.

The soldier had obeyed immediately, not doubting that the famous Luca had captured the runaway boson from an earlier trip. They had marched round into the funnel and into the cabin itself while the soldiers formed their phalanx outside.

Marco fixes his stare on Cadiz - the man to whom he owes his life. Luca is watching Pedro - the man who can, at any moment, alert the men at the ships and destroy Axa's plan. Both explorers have grabbed their swords and the friar clutches his crucifix. Toledo breaks the silence.

"Good afternoon gentlemen." He swings his legs off the bed and tries to stand. His voice is weak and even with the friar's help he can barely stay on his feet. "To what do we owe this honour?"

Marco keeps his arms aloft and switches his gaze gingerly to Toledo. "Governor, I bring news of a rebellion. The Calusa have turned against you and the Africans have seen their chance to be free."

Cadiz and Pedro look at each other in astonishment. The prisoner is talking out of turn and he is making a preposterous claim. Moments earlier, all the soldiers had jogged back into the funnel outside and were shouting just in front of the cabin, with the dust from their drills billowing in through the open windows.

Luca raises his arms like Marco, flopping the pistol from his fingertips. "It's not loaded," he looks towards Toledo.

With his sword, Cadiz hooks the pistol from Luca's outstretched hand while Pedro points his sword towards the two unarmed visitors.

"Sergeant, give me a report," Pedro shouts out of the window, without taking his eyes off the imposters.

"Sir, the Calusa are restless. They wait at the entrance to the fortress, but they are out of range," the sergeant stares intently down to the open end of the funnel.

"Restless." Pedro yells. "What in God's name does that mean?" He twists his sword towards Marco's face, and with flaming eyes and unnerving authority he grunts, "It takes just one volley of shots to call the men from the ships. Now you tell us exactly what is going on."

Cadiz and Pedro move around from behind the table and Marco keeps his eyes on Toledo, who is still standing with the friar wiping his sweaty brow.

"Governor," Marco squares his shoulders, "word has come to the Calusa from the Indian gatherings. Luca has tried to deny it."

"What word?" Cadiz shouts.

Luca replies, now looking at the dangerously angry Captain. "Word that the Indian passengers last spring were not lost at sea, but died of a terrible disease brought by the sailors."

Toledo, Cadiz and Pedro go into a temporary stupor, knowing that this whole colony, and any exploration of this new land, depends on the lie that they were lost at sea.

From the glare outside comes news.

"Captain Pedro, Dark Cloud wants to speak to you,"

the sergeant stutters out his words.

"Luca, you have done this," Cadiz mutters angrily to Luca, as he goes to the window on his side.

"I knew the lie of course..." Luca sticks his chin out, "...but my status rests with the success of this Mission, not its failure. If I have survived the plague, the shaman will see me as a traitor... so the story of disease must have travelled with other voyages in the south and west."

Cadiz barks at Luca. "You must tell the Calusa that the scourge travels with the slaves. Tell them about the demons that cut three sixes into their skin."

Luca looks him in the eye. "Captain, the Calusa know that the plague killed the Aztec before any Africans set foot there - and here, the sixes are spirals... meaning peace."

There is a fracas outside, so both Cadiz and Pedro duck and weave to see between the soldiers who are lined up across the front of the cabin, three rows deep. The Calusa are in a line fifty paces away across the entrance to the funnel.

"They are just out of range of our muskets," Pedro grunts to Cadiz.

Dark Cloud stands in front of them, but they all still have their bows unarmed across their chests and their arrows safely in their quivers on their backs. A military standoff has been established, with each group out of range of the other, at either end of the high-fenced killing ground. There is no sign of the Africans.

"Senor Luca de Chicora, Senor Marco de Serena," Toledo manages to say weakly, "gentlemen, take a seat."

Luca and Marco make eye contact with Cadiz and Pedro to seek their approval, before settling in the chairs they have vacated.

"What do you suggest?" Toledo asks, with the friar

still fussing over him as he sits on his bed next to the dinner table.

"May I?" Marco reaches for a chessboard and pieces that are gathering dust on a sideboard.

"By all means," Toledo waves his hand. "Though I might need the friar to make my moves very soon," he grumbles and signs a crucifix on his chest.

Marco places the set of ebony and ivory warriors on the table and the chess set mirrors the impasse outside. The lines of heavily-armed Spanish soldiers and Calusa braves observe each other exactly as the pawns do across the chessboard... out of range and waiting for the first move.

"Remove the African chains." Dark Cloud booms out in Spanish, shattering the stable but nervous truce outside.

Toledo reaches forward and fiddles with the chess King on his side of the board, tipping it over but not letting it go - as if contemplating resignation. Instead, he brings it to his mouth and blows the dust off its crown, before replacing it on the board.

"Governor, sound the alarm," Pedro pleads to Toledo.

"No." Toledo snaps. "I don't want unnecessary bloodshed. That would set back the Mission of San Miguel for years, perhaps forever."

Marco sees the soldiers pull their lowered muskets into their shoulders - the next stage of readiness before raising the weapons, taking aim, and firing. For now, whatever alarms them isn't enough to lift the heavy barrels. These are only raised to fire just before the leaden rain of death is poured onto its targets.

"Jesus Christ. What are they up to now?" One of the sergeants mutters, wiping his dripping brow with his sleeve.

"Sergeant, give me a report." Pedro's demand comes from inside the cabin.

"The killing-ground is lost," the sergeant shouts over his shoulder towards the cabin, but keeping his eyes forward towards the Calusa.

Indoors, Cadiz and Pedro take it in turns to look out through the rank and file of the soldiers - trying to see the activity at the far end of the wooden walls of the yard. What they see makes them grunt and shuffle angrily, as nothing in their training or experience has ever presented them with such tactics.

At the wide entrance to the fortress, Axa from one side and Kofi from the other side, lead the chained and unarmed Africans into a line in front of the Calusa braves.

Cadiz and Pedro exchange puzzled looks and the sergeant starts to sound panicked.

"Sir, what are your orders?"

TREACHERY

"Wait." Toledo shouts, mustering all his remaining breath.

The air in the cabin clings to their skin, while outside the sun is beating down, and the lines of fighters are cooking gently in the exhausting oven of the yard. It is a terrible time of day to fight.

The Calusa chant under their breath about justice for their lost family, and the Africans are gambling everything to get their freedom, now or never. They control the only entrance and exit to the fortress, while the Spanish explorers ask for a way home to Spain, or to heaven. Axa's prayer is jostling with all the others in the spirit-space... 'Ona, take Jay and let her lead the way.'

The Creators of all three peoples want peace, but death or festering wounds are now fated for most souls on both sides.

Luca and Marco face the friar and the three hardened explorers. A cockroach swaggers slowly across the chessboard and everybody is briefly spellbound by its brazen manner. At the table, Marco politely picks up a table knife, holding it sideways and using it to slide his whole row of chess pawns up to the half way line - within range of Toledo's pawns. A two-squared first move from the Governor will start the battle.

He looks calmly at the old man, whose dry eyes are still windows onto a clear and clever mind. A cheeky smirk forms in the folds of skin on Toledo's face.

Marco slides his entire row of major pieces up behind the advanced pawns. Toledo looks at Pedro, Cadiz, and Luca - who are all now looking at the chessboard. The military balance has changed and a full-scale attack would see the Africans take the brunt of the slaughter – but it would use up the space. Their hobbling human-shield would bring the Calusa within range to use their bows, and the Spanish advantage would be gone.

"Governor, if I may be so bold?" Marco glances out of the windows. "You can stop them... but we will all die."

This new reality is now clear on the ground outside, as well as on the chessboard inside.

"Let me kill him first," Cadiz insists. "I should have let him hang, back in Dominica. Now I can finish the job. Then Luca will die too, for protecting the Satan he was sent to kill."

Everybody looks at Luca, but he just stares out of the cabin into the sunlight.

"Captain, you took my life," Marco still looks into Toledo's fading eyes, but addresses Cadiz, "by sending me into exile. Now I am here to save your life. If you accept Dark Cloud's offer to leave, then we are even."

"You don't dictate terms to me." Cadiz spits, taking aim for his lethal strike. "Die now as a traitor." He raises his sword but Marco falls to the floor on his knees, head bowed before the friar.

"Stop," Toledo places his hand weakly over Marco's exposed neck and Cadiz's sword swishes harmlessly down by his side.

From outside, another call comes from the sergeant, this time more demanding and panicked.

"Sir, now what are your orders?"

Cadiz and Pedro go to the windows again and Marco glimpses the African line take one step determinedly forward, in death-defying unison. The Calusa bowmen step forward just behind them, man for man and woman for woman. 'One step at a time,' Axa had said on the way from the gathering - when she seemed to have no plan.

If the Calusa get closer, the soldiers would have only seconds to ready, aim and fire before the arrows rain down on them... but Pedro should give the order to cause so much death – and kill the unarmed people who saved so many from drowning. At least then, Captain Pedro would have to explain the injustice at the gates of heaven.

Here in the dying fields, the end will come quickly from terrible injury or slowly from infected wounds, so Axa has sent Chet and Jay to watch for any reinforcements from the ships.

She and Kofi stand in front, as the Calusa make their bows and arrows ready and the soldiers raise their muskets ready to fire. Axa has left behind both her knives and only her three-pronged weapon is still strung to her lower back for luck. One or two of the Africans make eye contact with the soldiers they rescued from the shipwreck. At the other end of the funnel, those soldiers gulp in horror at the thought of shooting those who had spared them from the alligators.

Axa wriggles her toes in the baking sand, feeling its caress for one last time. Her last memory in this life will be of biting that dust, when hit by the first volley of gunfire.

Still on his knees, Marco reaches to the chessboard and pushes his pawns forward another row of squares. They are now in Toledo's half, and Marco pushes all his major pieces, and their firepower, up behind them. The Governor's pieces look very cramped and useless.

"Sir," the sergeant bellows, still facing the enemy and steadfastly maintaining a professional attitude despite the mounting pressure from in front and the dithering from the cabin, "their leaders are in range of the first volley.

They will at least get most of that."

Axa cannot see beyond the rows of twitching
Spanish marksmen, but prays for Marco to break the
Spanish will - to offer them something – to make a
bargain that will compensate them for defeat. She closes
her eyes tight. Now Marco my brother... you must use
the spider and the clown. In God's name, use your saints
and your sins. You promised you could turn the friar and
Toledo. You must do it now.

Marco feels the Governor's palm on his neck and the old
man shivering to the marrow. "Friar Antonio," Marco
pleads in a last confession, "forgive me for I have sinned.
You both know my father, and the proud name of De
Serena. In the name of King Carlos, and above all in the
name of God... please forgive my soul."

The rows of Spanish soldiers outside close one eye and
take aim, and the Calusa draw their loaded bowstrings
back. Axa and Kofi wait for their limbs and organs to be
torn apart by gunshot.

Young warriors on both sides, with so much of their
lives before them, go weak at the knees. The older ones
have seen flesh-ripping and bone-smashing brutality
before. Having witnessed the randomness of death, they
stiffen as the others falter. The waverers see the example
of the veterans and pull themselves together - bonding as
a unit, but every man for himself. However skilful, all
their lives are in the hands of luck. The short panting of
the young settles to join the long, deep breathing of the
older fighters. Their fingertips tingle as blood courses
away to muscles, sweating stops, and red mist drifts in.
They will not need detailed memories of the blow-by-

blow events, and the caring parts of their minds will close down... becoming killing machines, ready to butcher others without thinking.

Marco offers Antonio his hand, which the friar joins with the Governor's free hand – holding them together in front. The priest holds the fate of the Catholic Mission, but he isn't a statesman or explorer. He is a route to God, and the souls of Toledo and Marco are poised before that almighty being.

Cadiz tightens his grip on his sword and again his elbow bends to deliver Marco's execution.

Outside, the soldiers curl their fingers around their triggers, and the Calusa's fingers loosen slightly on their tightly-stretched bowstrings. The Africans, including Axa and Kofi, squeeze hands and take another step forward towards the afterlife. Everyone, even perhaps Cadiz, makes one last prayer that some godly act will prevent bloodshed.

Friar Antonio looks into the Governor's closing eyes and nods acceptance of Marco's pleas.

"We must take him back into the Kingdom of God."

Toledo only hears the words that he wants to hear - 'take him back' - and belches out his dying words.

"Give them the keys to their chains."

SUCCESSION

A year after releasing the Africans, all the Santee clans have come together just as the matching moon is due to show. Chet watches quietly while a well-rehearsed routine of chanting is getting the festival started.

"Sergeant," Inca shouts in Spanish, perched on a rock in the middle of the village, "give me a report."

"The killing-ground is lost." A cheer goes up in the garbled Spanish of a hundred Santee and African voices.

"Sergeant, give me a report." Inca shouts again.

"The killing-ground is lost." The crowd bays again and falls about with laughter.

Once more, both Inca and the crowd bark out their repartee for the third and final time. Then a rousing cheer subsides, before the crowd settles down around the square and waits for the next part of the show.

The older children stand shoulder-to-shoulder to recreate the Spanish fortress, while the younger children line up in battle-dress and re-enact Axa's brilliant plan. It is a great honour to play the Africans, a slightly lesser honour to be the Calusa bowmen, and a punishment to play the Spanish soldiers. These poor souls get a battering from the toy arrows, which always get fired despite the famous truce.

Kuruk laughs with Chet and Kofi, "How does our most famous story of peace plunge into brutal chaos, every time it's acted out?"

The show has been practised every new moon after the legendary event, and after only twelve months it is part of the village folklore.

"Kuruk," Chet responds, "it makes my blood boil that we were not there to see it. Axa sent Jay and I towards the ships, to hold them back if necessary. If I had known about her plan, I would not have left her at the fortress."

"She promised me she would take no chances." Kuruk shakes his head.

Kofi then adds his thoughts. "My Santee language is still weak, but I can say that your Ashanti princess knew what she was doing. I would not risk my life for her, if I didn't know how clever she is." He gets his point across, mixing the spoken word with a few rich hand signals and expressions.

They watch the final stages of the re-enactment, where the lines of unarmed 'African' children step forward as one, and the 'Spanish' children raise their wooden muskets. Kofi grins from ear to ear, waiting for the shout of 'Release their chains'.

"How strange is fate," Kuruk smiles, "that my famous wife is missing this festival. Her waters have broken and she's deep in labour now, so perhaps the child will be born a year after the Africans were reborn." He puts a long arm around Kofi, who nods with delight at the idea of this stroke of luck.

The free Africans are the focus of the event but Kofi wriggles modestly at their fame. As the months have gone by, they have learned the language of the Santee and in return taken great pleasure in teaching them their language of the drums. Small drumming classes are taking place all over the forest and as the groups get more skilled they talk to each other. Sometimes the whole valley unites as one giant band of pounding beats and all the birds and animals sing or howl their part. As one build-up of drums shakes the ground and then dies down, Chet takes up the theme of parenthood with Kuruk.

"Prince Kuruk of the Santee," he pats him on the shoulder, "you should go to Axa now and in the Santee way you must be sweeping the tepee until just before the child is born." He has made up this ritual with Ona during the last weeks of the pregnancy, because Kuruk was fussing around more and more and needed something hearty to settle him down. His sweeping has already hollowed out the tepee floor.

Now in the early stages of labour, Axa takes her mind off things by meditating on recent events. Carrying the baby had gone well so far and village life had returned to normal, with the added twist that it now included African clans. The Santee have shared everything they have with their new cousins, and new courtships are blossoming between them as well as among the African clans. Fewer women came with the colony and they are courted all the time, while some African men are finding Santee lovers or looking for new land on their hunts, if that is their nature.

Axa's thoughts turn to her own blessings and Ona's early advice about motherhood. "Dearest Axa," she had said at the early stages of the pregnancy, "it is two moons after missing your period. Now we can tell the tribe that you are pregnant, if they haven't already guessed. We have certain customs involving midwives, close family members, and others with special roles in the tribe. They will all be very excited."

"Mother Ona, I am Santee now and I want all their blessings, but please include my African sisters or they will be very jealous."

"Of course. Now, in our custom pregnant women avoid eating raccoon or pheasant which could make the baby sickly... speckled trout can cause birthmarks and eating black walnuts gives the baby a big nose."

"Ha ha... " Axa had told Ona at the time... "The Ashanti think that lingering in doorways slows the birth."

She didn't have much time for witchcraft, but had stopped jesting when she had seen Ona's grave and scolding look. This Ashanti myth was a Santee belief too, but it was not a laughing matter.

Here in the birthing tepee, Nani and Nana wash Axa's hands and feet, and medicine-women perform rites that will make the birth easier. Axa's cramps are regular and very painful, as she practises the standing posture ready for the final stages.

"Axa my love," Kuruk adds mopping her brow, "in the Pensacola we have a ritual to frighten the child out of the mother's womb. One of your Ashanti sisters must say to the baby, 'Listen little one, get up at once, here comes an old woman.' That should do the trick. If it doesn't, I have made some tea of cherry bark to speed the cramps."

"You are very sweet... but if you stay any longer I will bite your fingers off."

Kuruk takes the hint, and takes the broom so he can sweep up outside the tepee instead. The first and second stages of birth are fairly swift, and the baby's position is normal when its head shows. The midwife simply encourages Axa's efforts while the others help her to squat comfortably. In turns, distress and total focus consume her, as the waves of energy wash through her body. Several more deep breaths and agonising pushes later, the baby girl is born.

"A daughter." is the chorus of praise from Ona, Jay, and the twins.

ABBY

In the Santee way, no one catches the baby, who drops onto a deep bed of leaves. Swooning, Axa lies back exhausted and the little girl starts breathing with the impact of the short fall. The midwife checks the baby and the cord, and passes the tiny new-born onto Axa's chest while she waits for the afterbirth. Axa laughs, weeps, and heaves in the baby's scent, while Ona and all the aunts praise her and the baby as the bravest and most beautiful creatures ever to grace the land. They allow Kuruk in and he begins doting on the two of them - cooing in the baby's ear and flaring his nostrils.

As a grandmother already, Ona cannot resist some more ritual.

"Darlings, we think the real parents are Corn Mother and Sun Father, and we mortal parents are only tools of these over-reaching powers." Nobody pays any notice, but she dutifully rambles on. "This ear of corn, whose tip ends in four kernels, symbolises the Corn Mother, to be kept next to the baby in darkness for twenty days."

Axa isn't listening and her new-born roots for the nipple. She has expressed some milk and wastes no time before this first sucking rehearses for feeds that are more frantic in the next few days. While she dozes on and off for several hours, the others wash the child in cedar water, then rub her in the finest white cornflour, and leave her like that for the rest of the day. Nani and Nana are exact in their rituals and they take turns in bathing and scrubbing the new princess. Nani proudly talks about the diary of washes and rubs.

"For the next four days we wash her and rub her in cedar ashes, to remove the hair and baby skin. We repeat the one cornflour rub and four cedar ash rubs, until four full cycles span twenty days - all in the darkness of the tepee."

Ona and Jay keep the tribal habits going, leaving Nani and Nana to focus on supporting Axa.

Nearby, Chet explains to Kuruk his assorted duties, such as making the cradle that his daughter will use for the first year. While Kuruk carves the backboard, Kofi comes to lend a hand.

"Prince Kuruk, it would be a great honour to help you carve some of the cradle."

"Prince Kofi my friend, it will be an even greater honour to make it with you, and this will seal your support for our marriage."

"I am not jealous. Axa and I were arranged to marry, but you two are in love. The blessing of a healthy daughter is a sign that it is meant to be, and now you must decide whether to give her three spirals."

"I hope you don't mind, but Axa has decided to defer to the Santee custom, and I confess that making marks on such a beautiful ebony forehead would be too difficult for me."

"I am happy to hear that. Your ideas for choosing your leaders make much more sense. Clearly we were lucky with Axa, but your process of choosing from the many royal grand-daughters is better... safeguarding the motherly line and making sure that the best queen is found."

"Kofi, you can be my daughter's uncle, because in our tribe a man's duty is to protect his sister's daughters, and less so his own children. Axa has no blood-brothers here and we will give you that tribute."

"That is our way too." Kofi beams. "A husband can die or leave, or women can change their minds. Uncles on the other hand may die, but they can never leave, so a mother relies on her brothers, whatever the future unfolds for her children."

"All-Seeing Eye, soon you and I can take the fight to the Spanish, and make sure that my daughter will never be a captive."

The smile falls off Kofi's face, and he quakes with fear. The devil just spoke in Kuruk's voice.

Chet sees Kofi's shock and shakes his head to dismiss the comment for now, while Kuruk returns to Axa in the tepee. Kofi holds the cradle as the symbol of the new baby's safety, but hears the chill wind of revenge echoing from Kuruk's lips. Chet can see his distress, so he quickly confronts it.

"Kofi my friend, the gods didn't free you from the Spanish, just to make you a prisoner of revenge. Here too, this is the devil that legends say will release a cruel cycle, ending in disaster."

Kofi looks at him through floods of tears, flowing as if he has been holding them back ever since his own capture, so far away. Chet forces home his point before changing the subject.

"Our brothers in the south have stories of the Taino tribes of the southern islands, saying they were wiped-out by fire… men, women, and children. Other stories of the Aztec wars and plagues have come from the Navajo in the west, so history is full of dire warnings, but we don't have to trust them."

Kofi wipes his eyes and speaks in hushed tones, "Who is starting these rumours?"

"Devil spirits. Don't worry… Kuruk and the Wichita boys are headstrong but it will pass. Have faith in the Three Spirals, and let's get back to the festival."

Axa is feeding the baby but Kuruk sees she has something on her mind.

"Axa, are you missing your friends, Marco and Luca?"

"Yes. Letting them leave with Cadiz may not have been the best choice."

"They convinced him and the friar that their duty was to them, and their safe return to Dominica. Chet watched them go back to the ships and says they were being fairly treated. Even if Cadiz and Pedro don't trust them, they do have to thank them for their lives."

"Kuruk, they bluffed the Spanish leaders but it was Dark Cloud who gave the Spanish no choice, and the best they could do was save face."

"Your friends Marco and Luca felt they could protect us better by being among the Spanish and it was probably the right idea."

"Something tells me our future safety is in their hands as much as our own."

"Axa, you may be right, but for now the future is our new baby daughter, and we need to decide on names. We should use the maternal grandmother's names... so another Ona, or my mother's mother. Whichever name is most used will become the name settled on over time."

"Remind me of your grandmother's name, on your mother's side."

"Abeekway."

"Kuruk, that's lovely. 'Ona Abeekway of the Santee' it is then. What does it mean?"

"Stays at home."

Axa mutters her praise and breast-feeds the little girl, while Kuruk curls up around them among the fur and blankets.

Before sunrise on the twenty-first morning, Axa picks up the baby and at last they leave the tepee, with Ona alongside. The tiny Abby is wrapped in swaddling clothes and bound tightly to her cradle, as her mother and her queen walk purposefully to the east - praying and casting cornmeal towards the increasing light. The great white disc of the sun clears the horizon, and the forest is strident with animal noise. Axa holds the baby up to Father Sun, and chants quietly as she passes the ritual ear of corn over her in four directions.

Queen Ona then repeats this, but with lips grimly pressed together. She slowly nods to Axa who grasps Abby's cradle from her, before Ona goes back to the tepee and the waiting aunts. The Ashanti queen forces herself at funeral pace to the same riverside where she had slain the bear a year and a half ago. With the animal's pelt over her shoulders, clutching her breath, she plunges the infant into the river and vows through tears to do this every morning for two complete cycles of the seasons.

"My dear Abby... bless the spirals... this ritual will give you strength, and you too will be a queen and a mother one day."